There is a disquieting quality to the short stories in this volume. Their rhythm mimics the abrupt tempo of lives cut short without warning. It is impossible not to identify with the helplessness of decent folks with families, careers, aspirations, and family homes that represent a lifetime of savings, who are casually annihilated by industrial warfare on one side, and atavistic fanaticism on the other. But for the accident of geography, that could be you!

　　—Shadia B. Drury, *Terror and Civilization*

Political satire and Baudelairean humor can be the only response to the treacherous political atmosphere in Syria. Anyone who dares tell the truth will face the sword of the Sultan, much like the tales of the Arabian Nights. Originally from Raqqa, once the capital of the Islamic State, Musa Al-Halool, professor and translator, lampoons the hypocrisy of the regime and the nature of power in pithy fables, utilizes folk-tales to comment on the domestic life of farmers in the countryside and offers insight into the lives of Syrians, seared by personal tragedy, in vignettes.

　　—Gretchen McCullough, *Confessions of a Knight Errant*

Knit together by a subtle coherence, the collection gravitates around one understanding: when the author speaks about animals, he does so not from a desire to avoid speaking directly about human monsters, but to unleash the power of the imagination to build magic-realist worlds, where it becomes more effective to mock and denude the enormous political crime against the Syrian people. Smart sarcasm seems like a crucial key to understanding the depth and narrative technique of Musa Al-Halool's stories. Sarcasm alone can express the horror of what's going on today in Syria where direct language fails to unmask the secret history of 'rats' and 'dogs.'

　　—Riad Nassan Agha, former Syrian Minister of Culture

The Dusk Visitor offers us a simple dream: that a son may have his body rolled-up at last in a rug that was owned by his mother.

—Duncan Lyon, *Sand, Paper, Stone*

Al-Halool's collection mixes satirical vignettes, political fables, and longer stories in a distinct melancholic narrative voice that interweaves penetrating representations of the current tragi-comic realities in Syria through modernist doubt, Western literary allusions, and Syrian folktales. The collection skillfully elevates the Syrian apocalypse to cosmopolitan heights.

—Jamil Khader, Bethlehem University

Dr Musa Al-Halool lifts the veil of various intricacies and social customs of traditional Syrian society. Several stories deal with the author's homeland in the Syrian countryside along the Euphrates near Raqqa, later the capital of the ruthless Islamic State. Other stories deal with the situation inside Syria during the war, and among Syrians forced to live in exile, far away from their original homes. The Syrian human factor, unknown to many outsiders, occupies a central role. The most difficult situations narrated in this collection of short stories are intermingled with a high degree of humor, making it a pleasure to read. Next to its literary merits, it is instructive to those who wish to have a deeper insight into Syrian society.

—Nikolaos Van Dam, *Destroying a Nation*

In an upside down world where facts are twisted until they lose their mooring in reality and government actions are driven by the personality of the Great Leader, those few who stop, think, and question face utter indifference at the best or ridicule and ruin at the worst.

—Scott C. Davis, *The Road from Damascus*

THE DUSK VISITOR

Stories
from Syria

Musa Al-Halool

Cune

The Dusk Visitor:
Stories from Syria
by Musa Al-Halool

© 2022 Musa Al-Halool
Cune Press, Seattle 2022
First Edition

Paperback   ISBN 978-1-951082-13-0

Please contact us for Catalog in Publication info:
www.cunepress.com

Credits:
Black and white drawings (at the beginning of each section of this book) and the painting that we have sampled for our cover are by Hassan Hamam, a painter who is originally from Raqqa, Syria. (https://www.facebook.com/hassan.hamam.9)

Musa Al-Halool composed most of the stories in *The Dusk Visitor* in Arabic and then translated them into English.

Syria Crossroads (a series from Cune Press)

Explore the Old City of Aleppo	Khaldoun Fansa
Jinwar and Other Stories	Sami Moubayed
The Road from Damascus	Scott C. Davis
A Pen of Damascus Steel	Ali Ferzat
White Carnations	Musa Rahum Abbas

Bridge Between the Cultures (a series from Cune Press)

The Passionate Spies	John Harte
Nietzsche Awakens!	Farid Younes
East of the Grand Umayyad	Sami Moubayed
Arab Boy Delivered	Paul Aziz Zarou
Music Has No Boundaries	Rafique Gangat

 Cune   Cune Press: www.cunepress.com

Contents

IV. THE REPUBLIC OF NAMMOURISTAN

V. NOTES

Editor's Note

Musa Al-Halool hails from the Raqqa province of Syria and has made his career as a university professor of comparative literature, a translator, and a creative writer at universities in Syria, Jordan, and Saudi Arabia.

After the outbreak of the Syrian Revolution in March 2011, Musa refused to support the Syrian regime in its brutal crackdown on civilian protesters—Assad's rooftop snipers picked off random demonstrators in the crowds below. Unlike some Syrian writers, intellectuals, and artists who supported the regime, Musa sided with the victims. In *The Dusk Visitor,* composed from 2002 to 2018, his characters, (other than those in the political fables) are ordinary Syrians who are simply trying to live their lives.

The US invasion of Iraq, the Syrian Revolution, and the rise of ISIS are more than a distant historical backdrop for this author. Musa's property in Raqqa was taken by ISIS. The US strategy in Raqqa as in Mosul was to minimize US casualties by waging war from the air. Instead of interdicting the limited number of ISIS fighters in Raqqa, in the summer of 2017 the US dropped bombs, destroying 80% of the city. Musa's home town is now rubble and his family dwellings are lost, which makes him more than a voluntary exile.

As for his writing, Musa was polishing and arranging the pieces in this collection even as Raqqa was under assault. At my urging, he added an opening section where he sets fiction aside and speaks to us directly about his life in Raqqa and his face-off with ISIS and the Syrian regime.

In the context of the current suffering in Syria, readers may be surprised at Musa's bitter complaints about the regime's indifference to his professional qualifications, which are exceptional. I have noticed this same tender spot among other super talented men and women from Syria. They have struggled to excel in their fields and then, too often, the Syrian regime will award choice positions in universities or government to loyalists without a spark of creativity. It is hard to weigh the issue of professional injustice in the same balance as military violence—except to note that when people in positions of authority are selected for talent, not obeisance, there may be a better chance of avoiding the problems that we see now in Syria.

It is only fair to note that Buthaina Shabaan, a long time adviser to Bashar Al-Assad and his father, is a woman whose credentials as a feminist and an author of merit are beyond assail. She is an an exception to the rule.

Musa's complaints, of course, are directed primarily at the big picture: He tacitly compares the leaders of many Arab countries and their gangs of followers to the fascists that Hemingway observed in Italy in the 1920s.

After telling us about his life in "Our Bitter Harvest," Musa then presents eight political fables in a section called "Ratistan." The third section, "Che Ti Dice la Patria?" contains thirteen satirical vignettes. The final section, "The Republic of Nammouristan," contains fourteen longer and more sober stories. The author explains:

> I presented the fables and vignettes at the beginning to serve as appetizers or digestives for the reader. At times I found that a theme discussed in a fable or vignette would emerge later with more detail. In other situations, a particular fable or vignette would also work nicely in juxtaposition or serve as a companion to one of the longer stories.

Taken together, Musa's short pieces and longer stories turn teasing into ridicule, a Biblical two-edged sword, that cuts through the lies, self-congratulation, and buffoonery of national leaders. Musa goes on to say:

> . . . in our Arab world, bedeviled by all manner of mediocrity and strife between the populace and the political kleptocracy, literary writing must be an act of resistance (by mocking the ruling dictatorships and denuding their stooges and brown-nosers), not just a purely aesthetic expression.

Musa's flaming rage mirrors that of writers such as Jonathan Swift. Closer to home, his caricatures in prose recall the most cutting visual art of Ali Ferzat, the famed Damascus political cartoonist who published a caricature depicting Assad hitching a ride from Gaddafi on his way out of town. In response, regime thugs kidnapped Ferzat from his home, crushed his fingers, and tossed him from a speeding car on the airport road.

Aside from Bashar Al-Assad and Egypt's Sisi who are still in power, Musa also lampoons Muammar al-Gaddafi of Libya and Tunisia's Ben Ali.

Sad to say, the obtuse mindset that Al-Halool pillories has now taken hold among the right in Europe and the US. American readers in particular will understand that these stories are not quaint or hypothetical. They are written for our time and our place.

The Dusk Visitor . . . is a cautionary tale. It warns us to treasure and to fight for the civic virtues we hold dear. Otherwise, we may well find that the bleak upside-down world of this book, drenched in public platitudes and private blood, is a vision of our own future.

"Che ti dice la Patria?" can be translated "What Does the Fatherland Tell You?" Musa Al-Halool has inserted a Fascist phrase that Ernest Hemingway used in 1927 as the title of a story set in Italy, two years after Mussolini became Italy's ruler. The connection to Syria?

Musa Al-Halool, first read Hemingway in elementary school and went on to translate the latter's complete short stories into Arabic—at the behest of the Kuwaiti National Council for Culture, Arts, and Letters. His favorite Hemingway texts when he teaches are *The Old Man and the Sea*, "Cat in the Rain," and "Old Man at the Bridge." The choice of this latter story is not surprising. Set in Spain during its bloody civil war, it foreshadows what millions of ordinary Syrians came to experience more than seven decades later (in the Syrian Revolution that began in 2011 and still continues). Also, events in Italy and also Spain are just across the pond to Syrians whose trading relations with Mediterranean nations have been strong since ancient times.

"Che ti dice la Patria?" is an Italian phrase that Musa uses to remind readers, especially Americans, of the lazy way that the world ignored the warnings of its writers following World War I and allowed the civic society developed in the West over a couple of centuries to be degraded, challenged, and ultimately overthrown by men who were experts at exploiting the fears of the citizenry.

Hemingway first came to Italy as a soldier in 1918. In 1922 he interviewed Mussolini and, in another article that year, commented that Italy's Fascist thugs "had a taste for killing under police protection and they liked it."

In 1937 Hemingway was in Spain during Guernica (pattern bombing by Nazi planes). He saw armed fascism up close: an elected government over-turned by the right, government supporters divided, throwing each other in front of firing squads. Those who escaped to France were returned to Spain in chains. Many spent World War II as Nazi prisoners at Mauthausen (Austria).

Hemingway warned us.

Musa Al-Halool sends regards to Hemingway. He offers *The Dusk Visitor* as a book end to Hemingway's political fiction from Italy and Spain. And he renews the warning that Hemingway raised about the threat of the weaponized right.

In *The Dusk Visitor,* word buffs may be interested to know, Musa Al-Halool plays with the suffix "stan." He gives us "Ratistan," "Nammouristan," "Repressistan." When I asked why, he explained:

> In modern Arabic literature, adding "stan" (meaning "land" or "country") to any Arabic stem will immediately invest the coined word with humor or sarcasm. If you call a place "dogistan" you are saying it is the "land of dogs" or the "land governed by people who act like dogs."

Musa also explained the "i" that Americans are used to with this construction. The author explained:

> Etymologically, the letter "i" has been added to such names as "Pak-i-stan" or "Afghan-i-stan" because of a phonetic necessity in Persian (the same applies to Arabic): inserting a vowel between two consonants (the coda of the stem and the initial of the suffix). By comparison, in names such as "Bantustan" or "Hindustan" there is no need to insert this phonetic bridge because the stem ("Bantu," "Hindu") already ends with a vowel.

In *The Dusk Visitor,* Musa Al-Halool identifies lands, governments, states, and states of mind that are utterly insane . . . complete nonsense. And yet everyone in these "stans" operates as though nothing is amiss. In an upside down world where facts are twisted until they lose their mooring in reality and government actions are driven by the personality of the Great Leader, those few who stop, think, and question face utter indifference at the best or ridicule and ruin at the worst.

—Scott C. Davis, *The Road from Damascus*

Preface

THERE'S A DISTINCT "VOICE" TO THIS BOOK, and it is one that I confess captured me from the very beginning. Even as I read the first story, I realized that we have here a writer who has all those qualities we expect in an author but rarely find in one person.

The most important quality is that there is absolutely nothing pretentious about Musa Al-Halool.

The second quality is accessibility. Musa shares his personal story and his fictional creations in a manner that obliterates distance. We are always with him. It is easy to visualize him happy, annoyed or simply having an inner conversation. Achieving this requires a talent that I, as a novelist myself, have often struggled with.

The third quality is what might be called "intellectual depth." The voice sharing these stories is one you want to trust because it often illustrates that it is educated as much as it is experienced. Attentive reading is not as easy for me as it once was, yet this book had me hooked from the start.

But there is far more in *The Dusk Visitor* than a distinct voice. One of the important layers to the ongoing Syrian tragedy that so-called Syria-experts, like me, often encounter . . . is just how difficult it has become to humanize the Syrian.

Syrians are refugees, survivors of oppression, radicals, fighters, violent or non-violent protesters. We are all this and more. But we are seldom if ever portrayed as regular people with normal human emotions, dreams, desires, and regrets. Reading Musa's book is essential precisely because its most powerful contribution, in my opinion, is the extent to which it succeeds in humanizing what has become far too objectified.

In *The Dusk Visitor* we encounter real people with real thoughts and feelings. We encounter the complex spectrum of Syrians—and to a lesser extent Arabs—that I know well, from the idealist to the oppressive, and from the simple and genuine to the complex and ingenious.

Finally, Musa Al-Halool's stories are important because they provide insights on how the Syrian tragedy has impacted the lives of Syrians. And something more: these stories are simple, yet powerful, and rise to the level of folk tale. Traditional Syrian folktales are rich in detail and powerful in resonance. They present the moral verdict of a Syrian community that includes those still living within national boundaries as well as our diaspora. These stories carry the skeptical glance of generations past.

I only wish my late sister, Muna Imady, who wrote *Syrian Folktales,* was alive to read this beautiful collection.

—Professor Omar Imady, Senior Fellow
Center for Syrian Studies
University of St Andrews

I
OUR BITTER HARVEST

A Personal Sketch

The Secret History of a Dog

Our Bitter Harvest

S HORTLY AFTER SUNRISE ON 30 AUGUST 2012, my eldest brother Muhammad arrived with a rickety van driver at my home, a two-story townhouse, in Raqqa. The driver was to whisk me, my wife, and three small children off to Aleppo Airport for our tenish-AM flight to Saudi Arabia, where I have been working since September 2002. The rickety van was no accident. In my garage, I had a brand new car, but it was too risky to have my brother or brother-in-law drive us in it for the 180-KM trip. Gangs and other hoodlums were very active in broad daylight on the highways since the outbreak of the Syrian revolution in March 2011. In the state of the resultant lawlessness, a good car would naturally be a decoy to further calamities, the least of which was to be kidnapped until ransomed. Raqqa, then hosting a few hundred thousands of refugees from other revolting Syrian cities and towns, was still the safest and most peaceful city all over the country. But it was not to be. In six months, it was 'liberated' by the Free Syrian Army and other then-affiliated factions. There was something ironic and fishy, however, in this dramatic *deus ex machina*. Though Raqqa was the last Syrian city to revolt, if it did at all, it was the first to be completely "liberated" in one blitz without even a show of resistance by government forces against the rebels. While some people naively celebrated, I was not so enthused. Be it a genuine liberation or a sly handover, it was inconsequential in military terms for the regime, securely bunkered up in Damascus hundreds of kilometers away. But I knew this event would simply unleash the regime's lust for more blood and indiscriminate destruction. In the years that followed, my worst fears were vindicated.

It is still my firm belief that the city, skirted by the formidable 17th Division and the 93rd Brigade on the north and a military airbase on the west, could not be so easily wrested by a few hundred lightly armed rebels with no noteworthy support among the local populace. By putting it up for grabs, Raqqa—always marginalized—was shrewdly calculated to serve as a Machiavellian foil to the so-called secularist Assad regime, which likes to dub all opposition, including George Subra and Michel Kilo—the two most visible anti-regime Christians—as Muslim Brothers. In due course, ISIS drove all other rebel factions out of the city and declared it the capital of its own puritanical Islamist Caliphate, with its own Salem-like trials and witch hunts.

For the regime, ISIS was a life jacket and manna from heaven, obscenely and self-servingly paraded before the Western media and international public opinion as the only brutal alternative for post-Assad Syria. And the ploy apparently worked, with the whole world now fighting ISIS to save Assad. It was then that the city witnessed the greatest exodus of its inhabitants to Turkey, Europe, the Americas. Clamped between ISIS on the ground and Assad's long-range scuds and other firepower from the skies, "Mere anarchy" was "loosed upon the world." ISIS berserkers, hailing from every corner of the planet, began scouring the neighborhoods of the city and lodging themselves in any house not inhabited by its own legal owner or renter.

My neighborhood, one of the swankiest in Raqqa, was officially known as Artists Quarter. But because a few top government officials had made it their home after retirement, it was popularly and humorously nicknamed Thieves Quarter. Some envious neighbor, a former government spy, kept nudging ISIS thugs to grab my house. Though my eldest brother had installed a number of people, mostly refugees from other cities, in it with fake rent contracts, it was finally requisitioned by a Tunisian or Libyan militiaman in early 2017, who looted its elegant imported furniture and appliances worth over US $30,000.

My equally beautiful country house, 50 KM due east of Raqqa on the northern bank of the Euphrates, fared no better. My brother Muhammad had fled to it when aerial bombardment on Raqqa proved too severe for his wife and children. A local ISIS rat informed the authorities concerned that "the apostate's house was illegally occupied by his eldest brother." Acting swiftly, some North African thug duly evicted Muhammad and his family and requisitioned the house. Luckily, the militiaman gave my brother till the next day to vacate the house, in which I had stacked about a thousand books, mostly in English—an anathema, nay, the very pink of apostasy! One conscientious nephew—who was later to flee to Turkey for dear life—smuggled the books to my youngest sister's and brother's under wing of darkness. The house was occupied the next day, and my late mother's studio apartment, appended to the house, was turned into a jail.

When the US-backed Syrian Democratic Forces began their campaign in March 2017 to liberate the countryside of Raqqa, my extended family fled to the desert north of our native village, where they lived in tents for months. As soon as ISIS fled the area, SDF seized my country house, de-mined it, and turned it into a military HQ. When the SDF liberators finally reached the outskirts of Raqqa in June, only several thousands had remained trapped in the city. The liberation was a Dresden-style affair, if only worse—with systematic destruction from the air and the ground to flush out the few hundred ISIS remnants. As the operation neared its end, 80% of the city was destroyed, including my beautiful residence, bought with the toil of so many years.

Yet this was not my only loss. On 27 April 2014, I received a WhatsApp message—then and still the main means of communication—from my brother Muhammad telling me that our mother had suddenly died two days earlier. Fearing for my life, none of my family, relatives, or friends advised me to go for the funeral. I could be either arrested by the regime for irreverently badmouthing it on Facebook, or by ISIS for choosing to live outside its jurisdiction (I was not yet convicted of apostasy). I had no choice but to stay put and watch the unfolding tragedy from a safe distance. In the meantime, I could put my pen to good use and contribute to the effort of other Raqqa expats—like the writer Dr Musa Rahum Abbas, author of *White Carnations*, and the painter Hassan Hamam (illustrator of this book)—to shed a bit of light on our beloved city's and country's open-ended tragedy.

***

During the academic year 1999/2000, I was teaching at a provincial private university in Jordan. I was poorly paid, lonely, and miserable. During one of my monthly visits to Syria, I was secretively approached and tantalizingly told by a former colleague (whom I will call Ayman) about an available top job in Damascus. Ayman encouraged me to apply after he had talked to the people in charge. He, then a junior diplomat in the Syrian Foreign Ministry, told me that there was a vacancy in the ministry and he wanted me to fill it. Officially and nominally, the job designation was called cultural advisor to the minister, but in reality I would be the personal interpreter for President Hafez Al-Assad—if I got the job, that is. I was also told that Dr Buthaina Shabaan, Assad Senior's interpreter then and Assad Junior's spin doctor now, had a falling out with the ministry and they wanted to replace her. Ayman's recommendation was irresistible. During my next visit, I was told that he had in fact nominated me and that I was welcome for an interview on 1 April 2000. I was not blind to the ruthlessness of the aging and ailing dictator, who was to die a few months later, but I did not mind being his personal interpreter—a moral blunder of which I shall be forever ashamed.

When I went for the interview, I was rudely received by the deputy minister, a certain Sulaiman, whose questions, or rather questionings, were clearly meant to discredit my qualifications as a translator. By the time I went for the interview, Dr Shabaan had apparently patched up with the ministry. The deputy's last question was if I was a member of the ruling Ba'ath party, and I said no. Sulaiman then told me that they would contact me. I left his office embittered not because I knew that I would not get the job, but because he, an ignorant but powerful man, had the nerve to question my qualifications as a translator. I never heard from them; nor did I ever ask Ayman, who was very apologetic after the interview, what happened.

I don't know what course my life would have taken had I succeeded in landing that job, especially now in light of the raging war in Syria, but I'm sure of two things: I wouldn't have translated about forty books so far, and you wouldn't be reading this collection of stories. My failure to get the job dispelled my briefly entertained illusion that one day my country would give more credit to qualifications than to connections. Two or three years later, I wrote "A Sojourner Reporting from Amman" in which I mixed the proceedings of my doomed interview with the deputy minister with events I witnessed or heard while teaching in Jordan. You see, sour grapes can grow into sweet fruit in due course. Now it is harvesting time.

Now a few disclaimers are in order. First, it is incorrect to lump all the stories in this collection as translations. For one thing, when an author translates his own work into another language, he feels he has more freedom than when he translates somebody else's. Therefore, I think it would be more correct to speak of "rewriting" than of "translating." I remember when I was still in graduate school at Penn State, I started translating the difficult novella of Rachid Boujedra, *Nocturnes of an Insomniac Woman,* from Arabic. As I grappled with the stream-of-consciousness technique used by the Algerian master with such finesse, I ran against many a hurdle in this Sisyphean task. So I sought help in the author's own French translation of the work. Even though my knowledge of French then was and still is limited, I was struck by the extent of changes Boujedra made in the French version. And so it is in my case, where I took liberty in making a few changes here and there. The elaboration on this point I leave to students of comparative literature, should anyone be interested in exploring the issue.

Second, three stories in this collection were in fact written in English. Why I chose English as my medium of expression in these stories remains a mystery even to me. I just felt like using English instead of Arabic, and I acted upon my impulse, without weighing the consequences or pausing to justify my choice. Therefore, I will neither attempt any detailed rationalization nor engage in shallow pedantry regarding the matter. However, it might be useful to mention that my first collection of stories and poems, *A New Grammar for the New World Order* (Amman, 2001), was in fact written almost entirely in English.

In the preface to the Arabic version on which the present collection is based, I stated:

I can't remember now why exactly I started writing in English. Perhaps I had found it easier for me to write in English, and, compared to my readings in English, those in modern Arabic literature were then rather limited. Or perhaps, the authority of internal censorship was far greater than the frivolous temptation of any creative impulse in Arabic. For I believed then, and still do, that in our Arab world, bedeviled by all manner of mediocrity and strife between the populace and the political kleptocracy, literary writing must be an act of resistance (by mocking the ruling dictatorships and denuding their stooges and brown-nosers), not just a purely aesthetic expression. Hence the biting sarcasm that prevails in this collection.

English had afforded me a modicum of safety and freedom of expression. But this freedom came with a price tag: oblivion. The sad fate of *A New Grammar for the New World Order,* now gathering dust somewhere in a dark cranny in a small publisher's storage room in Amman, was enough of a wakeup call. So, a few years after that doomed collection, I took to writing in Arabic, albeit cautiously. Suffice it to say here that my occasional reverting to English after that fiasco is either some mysterious atavistic slip or an expression of a greater censorial superego. But all caution was thrown to the wind after the outbreak of the Syrian Revolution on March 15, 2011. No subject was taboo anymore, and no recourse to cryptic symbolism or fabulation was necessary. And Arabic was naturally the preferred medium of expression.

Third, I must confess that I had entered the world of writing through the vicarious door of translation, which is a noticeable theme in this collection. I have always regarded literary translation, if carried out by a professional hand, not only as creative as—sometimes even more creative than—any original work, but also as a cathartic pursuit. Under repressive regimes, translation may also serve as a subtle or masked commentary on the target culture.

It was in the bleak December of 1999, when I suffered from loneliness in the small town of Jerash in Jordan, that I embarked upon the translation of Aesop's fables. It is true that my primary goal was, in the words of Edgar Allan Poe, to borrow "surcease of sorrow" from this cathartic engagement, I found some of Aesop's fables as relevant to our times as Ibn Al-Muqaffa must have found *The Panchatantra* when he translated the work into Arabic circa 750 AD as *Kalila wa Dimna*. The message of *Kalila wa Dimna* was not lost to the Abbasid caliph Al-Mansour who duly put Ibn Al-Muqaffa to death.

If the reaction of one reader of my translation of Aesop is any indication, the relevance of Aesop to our times was not lost either. A Syrian friend of mine, who read the book (published in 2001 in Amman), was understandably flabbergasted by my reckless adventure.

"*Docteur,* aren't you afraid of the consequences?" he asked.

"Why?"

"Well, there are many fables about the lion's injustice!"

He was of course alluding to the fact that a lion is called 'Assad' in Arabic and that any judicious reader would immediately see the verbal correspondence between Aesop's lions and Syria's Assads, father & son. My friend found "The Lion's Share" of particular political resonance to Syrians.

> A lion once went hunting with other beasts. They caught a fat stag. Nominating himself to divide it, the lion made three shares. He then declared, "I take this big share in my capacity as King of the Beasts; and I take the second share for having personally taken part in the hunt; as for the last one, well, let him take it who dares!"

Within months after the publication of my translation of *The Fables of Aesop*, I found another literary work of equal political import: *Party of the Deaf*, a novella by the Jordanian writer Fakhri Kawar. In the preface I wrote for the English version of the book, I made no bones about my goal in translating it:

> The moment I finished reading Fakhri Kawar's *Party of the Deaf* in Arabic, I felt like translating it. I have for some time wanted to write about the intellectual metamorphosis of slogan-mongering, wave-riding, self-righteous 'Shitheads' like Kha in our Arab world—for that is what the cryptic name of Kawar's antihero means. But I have neither the dedication nor the literary talent of Kawar. This English translation, therefore, is my vicarious vengeance upon Kha-like unscrupulous careerists.
>
> The totalitarian nature of our Arab regimes is bound to spawn such miscreants like Kha whose driving ambition is to move up the ladder of officialdom. In a world whose highest political virtue is toeing the party line and idolizing the local despot, all personal and national ideals, when put to the test, are thrown to the dogs. The octopic outreach of totalitarianism is felt when the schoolyard is turned into a recruiting center for government spies.

Being both a translator and a writer is like having a mistress and a wife at the same time, where one's affections are always divided. And just as translation may be an impetus to writing, it can also dull, numb, and eventually frustrate such an impetus. My desire to be a writer was on occasion blunted by my addictive involvement with translation. Here is a telling example: in 2009 I began writing a satirical novel whose immediate stimulus was a presidential decree issued by Bashar Al-Assad whereby violators who drove through a red light were to be fined the equivalent of US 500—more than a month's salary for the top paying jobs in the public sector, including those of university top ranking professors. In angry reaction to this unreasonable punitive measure, I posted a comment, under my then favorite pseudonym Hafyan At-Tayih (The Barefooted Wanderer) on a government-sponsored website called "Syria News" in which I sardonically recommended a return to the idyllic age of camel transportation, listing the practical, environmental, and sustainable merits of such a return. Later on I wanted to use this sardonic comment as the basis for a novel I tentatively titled *The Republic of Camelistan*. I made a workable outline and wrote about twenty-five pages, but then I was suddenly whisked away from my novel by an urgent translation project. Since then, the typescript has been gathering dust—or is probably now lost. The same goes for my scholarly work on the anthropomorphism of mountains in Arabic and world cultures.

Then came 2011, my veritable *annus mirabilis*. It was the year when the Syrian people rose against a 40-year old dynastic dictatorship, and the desire to write free of fear and censorship, fanned to greater flames than ever before, finally and irrevocably took hold of me. That same year I was invited to give a lecture on pseudo-translations at the Sheikh Sultan bin Zayed Media and Culture Center in Abu Dhabi. I was a VIP state guest, royally treated and handsomely rewarded. It was also the year when I hooked up with the Abu Dhabi-based Kalima Translation Project, the Arab world's greatest translation project, which published eleven of my translations so far, most of which were commissioned by Kalima itself. It was also when Al-Jazeera Media Network by sheer accident discovered my translation skills, as demonstrated in one of my translated books, and asked me to freelance for them—my very involvement with Al-Jazeera, even in the innocuous capacity of a freelance translator, was tantamount to high treason in the eyes of the Assad regime and its brown-nosers.

Now to a bit of background on the stories of the collection. "Our Father Who Art in the Vatican" was inspired by an unpleasant encounter I had in 2002 with a mediocre versifier who thought he could use his connections with the ruling Ba'ath party—a branch of which was operating at Tishreen University with which I was still affiliated—to sweet-talk me into translating a silly bombastic poem he recited in Arabic in the presence of Pope John Paul II when he visited Damascus in 2001. "An Account of a Good-for-Nothing Thug" is a mixed bag of facts and fiction; in it I recall, from the post-2011 vantage point, certain events from my days in elementary school. "Season of Migration to Switzerland" is based on a dream I had in June 2011, that is, in less than three months after the outbreak of civilian protests in Syria, and was published in an Algerian cultural and literary online journal called Aswat El Chamal (Voices of the North). The story turned out to be strikingly prophetic in the sense that what I had seen in the dream and what I had jotted down in the story came to parallel the course and complications of the Syrian Revolution later on.

With the exception of a very short story I published in a Jordanian weekly in early 2002 (now I can't even remember the title of the story or what it was about), I did not attempt to publish any of my stories in print until I wrote "An Account of a Good-for-Nothing Thug," published in the Lebanese quarterly *Al-Adab* in 2013. Getting the story published in this prestigious review boosted my spirits, though the same review had already published two studies of mine: a linguistic one on bloopers native speakers of a given Arabic dialect commit when speaking outside their local speech community. The other was entitled "Sexual Rhetoric of the Syrian Arab Spring" (available also in English on the Internet), exploring how both the Syrian regime and its opponents equally resorted to the time-honored sexual vilification gimmicks to discredit and tarnish each other. Al-Adab, however, rejected "Lost Snails," which was originally narrated in the first person. It is partly based on real incidents that took place either in Taif (the city of my residence in Saudi Arabia) or in Raqqa (my hometown in Syria) in 2011 and whose heroes were my own children.

Some of the longest stories were never published in any media, electronic or print. In "The Swirl" I recall certain real incidents in my life as a young boy doing some agricultural work during the summer. The use of the suggestive name Naji—which means "survivor"—contains a situational irony where this fictional character is the only one who dies—rather tragically—during a supposedly happy holiday. Part of the fiction in it was inspired by Mary Lockwood's story "Paul" (which I also translated into Arabic).

"Retired for Good" is based on an anecdote a friend of mine told me about a canine in our native village; "The Secret History of a Dog," begun in 2009 then neglected for five or six years before it was picked up again, is also based on an anecdote my brother Sayyed told me about how dogs in our village made a pact with wolves whereby the latter were allowed to raid sheep pens in the village provided that dogs received a share of the loot. In both of these anecdotes, I saw the potential of turning them into sardonic political fables. "Gilgamesh and the Young White Elephant" is based on a story I heard from a dentist friend. The events of the original story took place in Lattakia during the French occupation of Syria (1920-1946), but in my story they were set in the ancient Babylonian city of Uruk to comment on the current Arab supine capitulation to Iran's aggressive expansionism (particularly in Iraq, Syria, Lebanon, Yemen, and the Gaza Strip). "Inauguration," written in 2016, is also loosely based on an anecdote I heard in 1996 from my brother Muhammad about one of our Machiavellian distant relatives who had shrewdly played the political card to silence the very man he had wronged.

"Summoned to the Booth," "Love Meter," and "Dew and Rain" were written in English. "Summoned to the Booth," written in 2012, is 100% real. I only changed the name of the vice-president of the university in the story. "Love Meter," written in February 2017, was inspired by a computer game my eldest son had learned at school in 2010. But the story, which is pure fiction, is set against the backdrop of the Syrian war which broke out in 2011. The jittery shell-shocked wife, suffering from a deep psychological scar, can be a veritable Hemingway character. The last story, "Dew and Rain," written in March 2017, is nearly 90% real, the rest is pure fiction. Written as a news story in the first person, it was inspired by the events that followed the storming by the US-backed Syrian Democratic Forces of my native village on 12 March 2017, supposedly to liberate the Raqqa province from ISIS, and the subsequent flight of my entire extended family to the desert.

Finally, the reader will notice a bit of fabulation. This is partly a throwback from the self-censored period during which I wrote, and partly a reflection of my translation interests in world fables and mythology: the fables of Aesop, American-Indian tales and legends, Maori and African myths.

—Musa Al-Halool
  Taif, Saudi Arabia
  January, 2022

II
RATISTAN

Eight Political Fables

Retired for Good

Ratistan

Being a faithful transcript of a clay tablet, written in hieroglyphics, discovered in the North African desert.

IT IS SAID THAT IN THE BEGINNING of creation, rats were nomadic rodents, scavenging the earth for herbs to nibble on. With herbs being scarce, rats would spend the best part of their days gathering just enough to keep them alive. Because of this cholesterol- and triglyceride-free diet, and the unavoidable jogging, rats were slim and lived long lives. But no one knows how or why the first rat died, especially since he was in the prime of youth. His brothers and cousins raised a great lament. When the condolors left, and the great ad hoc funeral hole—dug especially to accommodate the hordes of comforters—was dumped with earth again, his brothers were at a loss as to what to do with him. Their eldest said, "Let me eat of my brother's flesh that I may gain more strength and youthfulness." Now since he was the Supreme Chief of Rodents, his words were orders. When he nibbled at the stringy thigh of his dead brother, a current of rapture shot through his body, and a tremor of terror through every other rodent present.

The next day, he went out, as was his habit, to answer nature's call and was surprised to see that feces, not droppings, came out of his bottom. He strode triumphantly back to his folks whom he assembled hurriedly and addressed them thusly, "I am your supreme chief, so hear ye me. I will put a fence around this desert of yours, and will call it Ratistan. I will build a health center, a school, and a number of jails for you. There will be no more grass, for ye shall eat each other. So listen to these my words, and disobey me not. I will make of this Ratistan the envy of all rodents." Then he dismissed them and sat down to write the constitution of Ratistan, which he named The Yellow Book, on account of the color of the ink in which it was written, an ink whose chemical formula scientists have failed so far to decipher. When he finished writing the constitution, he also composed the national anthem of Ratistan whose opening line goes like this:

Come, ye, Company of Rats, let's live no more like Rats!

It is said this was the first line of verse ever composed by a rodent on earth. Then the Supreme Chief of Rodents took a piece of cloth and made of it a flag on which he painted a throne carried by four small mice, while on the right and left of the throne stood two ferociously grimacing rats. Later on, archeologists found that the flag had been made of a primitive diaper that gusty winds must have flung over the fence into Ratistan.

Being imitators by nature, humans, pace Aristotle and later anthropologists, began to imitate this pioneering ratty experience in nation-building. They drew borders, took flags, raised armies, and built jails. Industry flourished (especially barbed wires and cinder blocks), commerce and foreign investments grew, and rodents were the biggest investors in the real estate sector in human societies.

According to chroniclers, after a while a series of earthquakes shook human societies, and one of their immortal leaders thought that rats had dug tunnels in his lands (for the purpose of smuggling goods to and from his country without paying custom taxes), so he ordered his underlings, "to arrest all rats!" When the Chief of Ratistan heard this declaration of war, he was shocked by this human ingratitude, which he immortalized in the following verses:

> Oh, the ingratitude of one I raised like mine own son!
> With these mine own hands I used to feed him anon.
> Many were the times I have taught him statecraft,
> And the first chance he has he stabs me like a brat?Many
> were the times I have taught him to versify,
> But to mock me he has all skill and craft to apply?

[N.B. The bottom of the clay tablet on which the above account is given is broken, there are missing lines, and the rest is unreadable.]

The History of a Sly Fox

A FOX PROPOSED TO A MAIDEN JACKAL IN MARRIAGE, but her family rejected him because he was known for being a trickster. Abu Al-Hussayn—the generic epithet of all foxes in Arabic—produced a document from the district chief testifying that he "genuinely repented and mended his old ways." None of the jackals dared to refuse this groom, because to reject him meant rejecting the testimony of the formidable district chief. And thus the jackals went against their tribal customs and married their daughter to this stranger, despite the disparity in tribal status between foxes and jackals. Her mother pulled her own hair, rent her face, and screamed in protest, but her husband said, "Silence, you brainless woman! Marriage is a matter of *kismet!*"

Things didn't go well between Abu Al-Hussayn and his good wife. Whenever he stole a chicken, he gave his wife the neck and wings, while he ate the rest. Whenever she left him and went sulking to her parents' house, they returned her to him in order not to anger the district chief. Desperation finally drove her to burn herself, and Abu Al-Hussayn fled his homeland to escape the revenge of his in-laws and the fury of his district chief. He came to a hill over which cats and dogs had a bloody dispute. He pitched his tent there and named it The Universal Bureau for Integrated Solutions, or UBIS for short. Among the services he advertised were the following: marriage counseling, engineering consultancy, state-of-the-art finishing, exorcism, graduation projects, cupping, spinster matchmaking, revitalizing the impotent, in vitro fertilization, hemorrhoids treatment, bikini waxing, religious incantations, customs clearance, real estate management, ghost writing (MA and PhD theses), seasonal rentals, court testimony, Botox injections, circumcision (males and females), slimming, poultry farming, and 4G WiFi.

Cats were waging a war of attrition against dogs, and both parties were too busy. None could visit Abu Al-Hussayn's UBIS to enjoy the luxury services offered there. After a long period of waiting, during which despair began to gnaw at his heart, it occurred to him to invite both warring factions to a peace conference to end the war between his neighbors and to give his business a chance to take off. He chose "Peace Is Cool" as the theme of his prospective conference.

Cats held a general assembly to discuss Abu Al-Hussayn's invitation. In attendance was a retired cat, well versed in classical rabbinic literature, who stood up to speak to the assembled people. "I don't know why I don't like the invitation to this ominous conference, but I know for sure that foxes belong to the canine family, and as the Arabs say, a dog does not step on or bite his own tail."

Laissez Pisser

IT IS SAID THAT THE ANCESTOR OF DOGS did not urinate like today's dogs, but rather like the rest of animals. One day, however, this dog was urinating next to a wall and did not notice that it was about to collapse. He hardly emptied a quarter of his bladder when the wall fell and killed him. He died before he could savor that sense of relief all creatures have after micturition. From then on, according to one historical account, dogs began to prop the wall they piss on with one of their hind legs. If it doesn't prop up a collapsing wall, it can at least forewarn the dog of its impending collapse in due time to escape. That's why today's dogs do not listen to human warnings scribbled on walls all across our fair country, "Don't piss here, you dogs!" After all, dogs know what's best for them, and survival is for the fittest and the strongest. This being the law of natural selection, it is quite natural then for dogs to establish the Canine Front for Barking and Heckling to defend dogs' natural and acquired rights, including their right to piss anywhere they like in our land.

Retired for Good

OUR VILLAGE HAD AN AGING DOG who lived a quiet life, disturbed by nothing. Before retiring, he worked in security. After retiring, however, he became President of the Society for Consumer Protection, the Supreme Leader of the Coalition of Barkers, Chief of the Canine Society for the Defense of Human Rights, and the Assistant Secretary of the Pan-Canine Society of Filibusters. Altogether, these responsibilities weighed down on him in due course and sapped the remainder of his once robust energy. So he announced through his official mouthpiece, K-9 Gazette, that he would withdraw from all public life and resign from all his official posts in order to make room for the young bloods to assume their roles in the present and future life of the village. And so he started to pay house-to-house courtesy visits, mooching from alley to alley. He would also visit the sick (even if they belonged to the enemy family of cats—this was just to discredit Peter Porter, that uppity author of "Mort aux Chats"), congratulate those just discharged from their compulsory military service, attend weddings, and bark a croaking farewell to the dead.

One day, he saw a pack of young dogs chasing a bitch, each trying to win her attention and amorous favors. The superannuated dog also wanted to attend this competition—though only in the simple capacity of Observer of the Proper Application of Canine Matrimonial Rules. But the young dogs chased him away—quite gruffly and rudely. He found a deserted wall nearby to lick his wounds on. When he saw a young dog mounting the bitch, the retired comrade uttered a sigh of sorrow over a national service now unappreciated. It cut him to the quick to see those ingrates snubbing him like that. Jealousy ate his heart out when he saw a brat of a puppy, young enough to be his own grandchild, mounting the jewel of his nation, before all dogs to see, without any respect or regard for seniority. He mounted the wall and uttered his last memorable sentence history will preserve for posterity, "Noaaaaaaaw, I understand you!" And then he involved himself in a series of gyrating motions, mimicking dogs during their harrowing coitus. In the meantime, while the gyrations were bringing him slowly to the end of the wall, he was barking painfully and attempting to express his anguish in verse, which he was never good at anyway:

It becomes superannuated love aspirants to hold onto every decaying wall.

To have his history of glorious service forgotten by the youth is understandable, but to be thusly disregarded by the jewel of the canine race is something he has never imagined. He recalled the verses in which a graying lover complains of being jilted by his young paramour. By recalling the love complaints of other sufferers, he wanted to comfort himself, and thus continued his gyrating motions, and shedding hot tears to cool off his anguish. Had he had his former powers, he would have thrown them all in jail on charges of contempt of the Supreme Canine Being. But he was no longer in charge of things, defrocked for good. He kept barking, gyrating, and retreating until he unwittingly fell on his back. The rest of the comrades continued their untroubled celebration of the canine wedding.

SOS

ATATTERED RAG WAS CAST NEAR A COLLAPSING WALL, and stayed there for some time. Hyenas used to answer nature's call on it at night, and during the day cocks kicked it around to amuse themselves. The rag was happy with its own *kismet* and lot. A gusty wind rose and cast it in an arid valley. Hyenas missed it at night, and cocks in the morning, but when they heard its SOS, they formed a joint rescue team that reunited the rag with the wall, which they now bolstered for free.

A Trial

"Your Honor, there stands before you today a treacherous infiltrator . . ."

"What's her charge, Councilor?"

"Aiding terrorists, Your Honor."

"How?"

"Supplying them with eggs, Sir. Last February this traitor laid and donated all twenty-eight eggs to the terrorists and . . ."

"Objection, Your Honor! February was twenty-nine days this year!"

"Do you have anything to prove your innocence, you wicked traitor?"

"Yes, Sir. Sir, I am a cock!"

"In the Name of the People, this session is hereby adjourned until the defendant hen's sex is determined by a veterinarian doctor."

The Puppy and His Shadow

In the prime of his naïve, tender youth, a pampered carefree puppy was cavorting westward, dreaming rosy dreams, equally enchanted by love songs and the warbling of nightingales and sparrows. Shortly before the final sunset, a gentle breeze rose and stroked his ears and coat. He turned around to see them reflected in the eastern mirror of shadow. He was stunned to notice that the shadow of his tail was taller than that of his own, and he bit it off. Then the whole world grew dark in his eyes.

The Butterfly's Revenge

Mr Tough Guy walked into the bathroom to empty his bursting bladder. He spotted a brightly colored little butterfly circling above the half-filled toilet bowl. Aha, why can't answering nature's call be fun as well? When the butterfly came within good shooting range of his urinary firepower, he shot it with a volley that sent it tumbling down the bowl. It shook off the spray of his urine and flew, but he strafed it with another volley. It tumbled and he shot it again. Before Mr. Tough Guy could push the lever of the cistern to flush the butterfly down the drain, it managed to fly out and away.

He came out of the bathroom, having had his fun and relief, and no one could stint him the right to be flushed with victory. He stood washing his hands at the washbasin. He felt something sticky landing on the tip of his nose. He looked up at the mirror only to see the carefree butterfly frolicking there. Gripped by fury, he punched himself so hard on the nose, crushed the butterfly, and broke his nose bridge for good measure. The entrails of the butterfly, now mixed with his own blood and urine spray, slid down his upper lip, and with an involuntary flick of the tongue he licked them clean.

III
CHE TI DICE LA PATRIA?

Thirteen Satirical Vignettes

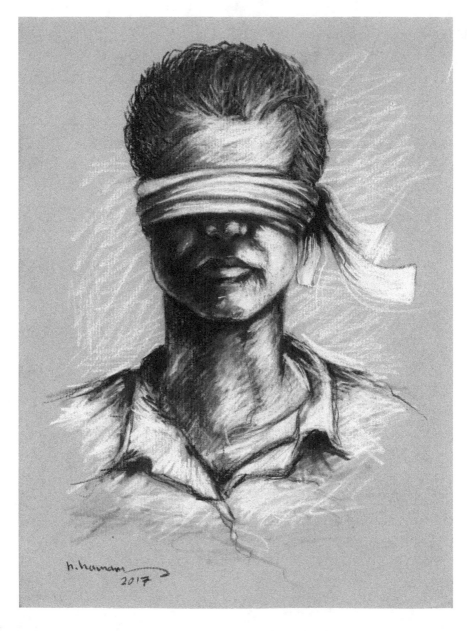

The Charge

Foster Brothers

A QUARREL BROKE OUT BETWEEN TWO FOSTER BROTHERS living under the same roof. One of them stormed out of the house angrily, but left the key in the keyhole from outside to prevent the one inside from getting out. When his anger subsided and he came back, he found that his brother had bolted the door from inside to prevent him from getting in. He went to a locksmith named Istafan, hoping he would persuade his foster brother to open the door, or else he would have to seek the help of whoever is willing to break into the house in which his brother was entrenched / imprisoned.

An Unfortunate Accident

A SYRIAN MAN DIED A NATURAL DEATH, and his relatives were immediately interrogated by the authorities concerned to find out the circumstances of the unfortunate accident.

Barter

A SYRIAN BABY WAS BORN IN A GOVERNMENT HOSPITAL and was welcomed by an official delegation. The baby sneezed, then praised the name of God and thanked Him. The head of the delegation approached and asked him how it feels like to get out of "the darkness of the womb into the light of the homeland." The baby wistfully said, "We had a good life." With tearful, grateful eyes, the head of the delegation said, "Bless the belly that bore you! We shall give you a nanny goat to suckle you, but in return we shall take your mother in National Defense."

National Dialogue

"You stole my watch!"

"How dare you! Don't you have any manners?"

"Then, what do you call your taking my watch from me by force?"

"That is not stealing."

"What is it? Tell me!"

"It is a simple transfer of ownership from you to me without your knowledge or approval."

"Pardon me. I didn't realize things could be seen under a different light."

"Never mind. Do you want to buy it back?"

"How much?"

"How much did you pay for it in the first place?"

"A hundred dollars."

"Ok. I will sell it back to you at no profit."

The Quarter's Gate

OUR NEIGHBORHOOD SAID TO THEIRS, "Your 'Valiant Eagles' raided our neighborhood, destroyed the bakery, and killed a number of civilians, including a pregnant woman who happened to be passing in the street at that time."

One of theirs replied, "Our army has no air force." "Such is not the moral behavior of our military!" said another. One whose sister used to come back home at 3:00 am retorted, "Perhaps, that woman conceived out of wedlock and was thus duly punished by God!" The gray fence-sitter said, "Now it is time for the replay of yesterday's episode of The Quarter's Gate."

Equal Opportunity

"MY GOOD SHEIKH, ONLY A FEW DAYS are left before the end of Ramadan. When should we pay the fasting alms?"

"To which sect do you belong, my son?"

"I'm from . . ."

"You're infidels. Neither is your fasting acceptable, nor should you pay fasting alms!"

"Oh sheikh, that's precisely what our own sheikh says about your sect."

An Account of
a Führer Extraordinaire

GOOD CITIZEN ABU SHALLAKH THE AMPHIBIAN gave us a true account of a sultan nicknamed 'The Pride of All Time.' Here below is a summary of his account. "When his mother gave birth to him, he spoke to the consortium of doctors in the maternity ward—each in his/ her own tongue; finished college in economics, political science, and law at the age of thirteen, earned three PhDs before he was fifteen; prayed his dawn prayers with the isha ablution for forty straight years; napped last Ramadan just before breakfast time, and the sun tarried for two hours before it set—just to humor him; during his felicitous reign no citizen drove through a red light, no tire was punctured, and no stray cat was accidentally killed; when he assumed power, precipitation rate jumped, the desert bloomed, and fountains gushed forth in the waste land so that all people had their own private fountains; during the first ten years of his good rule, life expectancy rose, death rate dropped to zilch, and the Grim Reaper stopped visiting our lands for good."

Repressistan

NATIVE SON DID NOT ATTEND A QURANIC SCHOOL, regular school, or university. Yet he was consulted by our townsfolks, even by the educated among them, to solve intractable problems. He was also quite popular because of the tales he tells, tales dating back to the age of legends and miracles. One of his quaintest tales was about a people living in another planet (though we know of no people in other planets). Pace Native Son, there was a country called Repressistan that had a master physician. This doctor was so authoritative that no other doctor, he being their chief, dared to treat any patient unless by a personal referral from him. It is told that a man took his boy, who suffered from chronic depression, to one of these doctors, who was also a relative of theirs. After examining the boy, and running a few tests, the doctor assured the father that his boy had an excess of black bile, an easy one to treat. But he advised the father to take his son to the Chief Doctor, just to respect the customs operative in Repressistan.

The father took his son to the Chief Doctor, accordingly, and after a long wait (there were too many patients), it was their turn to go in. The Chief Doctor asked, "What's your son's complaint?" Instead of describing the symptoms of his son's condition, the father blurted, "Black bile."

"Black bile? How did you diagnose his condition? This condition is unknown in our land. Have you taken your son to another doctor."

"Yes, to a relative of mine."

"Clannish solidarity!"

"Pardon me, doctor?"

"I said your son needs an urgent surgery."

"Is it necessary, doctor?"

"Of course! It is contagious."

"God's will be done. Do what you see fit."

Four hours later, the Chief Doctor came out of the operating theater, beaming with triumph, though visibly fatigued. The anxious father of the bilious boy rushed towards him, "How did it go, doctor?"

"It went well, thank goodness."

"And my son, how is he now?"

"Your son? May he rest in peace!"

Mediterranean Sweepstakes

O NCE UPON A TIME—in the twenty-first century AD to be precise—the Mediterranean Sea was until then called Mare Nostrum. This Mare Nostrum, claim oceanographers, used to gorge himself on the bodies of African refugees fleeing their countries to Europe. After a while, the sea began to complain of a heartburn and indigestion. He went to see a famed doctor on his eastern shore, who advised him to try the white Syrian flesh. Syrians, ladies and gentlemen, are part of a people who used to be called Arabs. These are now all extinct. Swallowed by history.

According to chroniclers, after trying this delicious diet, the sea's condition improved, his cheeks were rosy, and blood rioted again through his veins. In a moment of tranquility after a sumptuous feast on children's flesh, the sea noticed a Russian barge plowing his waves, and he wanted it to carry a long message of gratitude to that master physician. But it was cruising to his eastern shore with a lightning speed, so he only managed to improvise this hemistich:

I'm the SEA in whose bowels all shall perish . . .

The barge didn't wait for him to finish his effusions, but he saw an Iranian warship coming from the Sea of Qulzum, and before it had time to slip to his eastern shore, the sea managed to concoct another hemistich:

Oh, pray, give my love to that master physician!

It is also said that upon hearing this rhythmic speech, the Arabs were so over-joyed and mirthful that they took to dancing and singing. They composed measured, rhythmic phrases they named verses. And in gratitude to the Sea of Munificence—aptly named the White Mediterranean in Arabic, because it had white hands in mediating and diffusing the inevitable conflicts between the two barges—they named these metrical measures "Seas of Verse." They kept dancing, singing, and improvising verses until a coquettish wave came and swept them off their dancing feet and flung them into the bowels of the sea, where they joined their Syrian brothers and sisters who have already tasted the bounty of these Mediterranean sweepstakes.

The Charge

I WAS BROWSING THE INTERNET one late Thursday night / early Friday morning, when four gunmen broke into my house, blindfolded me, and led me to an unknown destination. I don't know how long we drove before the car stopped, and I was told to get off and was then led to a dark basement, where I was immediately interrogated. The men were a Russian, a Frenchman, an Englishman, and an American. I asked them about my charge, and they said, "Plotting a terrorist act." The silly charge made me laugh.

"Aren't you from Raqqa?" they asked me.

"Yes," I said.

"Why were you looking for Moulin Rouge?" the Frenchman asked.

"How did you know I was looking for it?" I asked him.

"Oh, we've been keeping track of your internet browsing, and it seems that you have been planning a terrorist act. You are from Raqqa; you must have a motive to respond to our war on terrorism."

And the Englishman said, "What business have you got with London Eye? Are you planning to blow it up?"

A similar question came swiftly from the Russian, "Do you intend to kill Daria Kondakova? Blyat! Why have you all of a sudden become interested in this gymnastics medalist?"

As for the American, well, he asked me this, "Why have you been looking for pictures of the uniform of special forces?"

I told them, "Sirs, I'm only a translator, I carry no weapon but this pen. I'm currently reading a collection of Syrian tales by a friend of mine, who also happens to be from Raqqa, and I'm thinking of translating his collection into English—should anyone in your own world care to know about the tragedy of Syrians." They asked me about the name of my friend, but I was too confused and scared to remember it. After some strained effort, I told them, "His name is Abu Anwar." The Russian, who spoke Arabic well, said, "This can't be a writer's name. We want his real name." After some time, I don't know how long it was, I said, "Oh, his name is Musa Rahum Abbas, and his book is entitled *White Carnations.*"

The Frenchman pouted as if displeased by the title. The American asked, "And what has your friend's book to do with all these suspicious things you were looking for?"

I said, "All these things are mentioned in his book, and I wanted to know what they were and how they were spelled in English, in case I wanted to translate the tales, and I have never read about or heard of these things before."

Then I felt a hand reaching to my chest and shaking me gently. "Papa, Papa, wake up. It's time for Friday's prayers. Aren't you going to pray today?" I looked at my little girl's face and told her, "I'm afraid they'd accuse me of terrorism." My girl looked up at my face, not making sense of what I have just said.

The Dusk Visitor

IN THE LONG WINTER NIGHTS, Abu Imad began to miss the warmth of his wife's lap, recalling all their amorous escapades which they code-named "Crossfire" when they spoke of them with relish in front of the kids the following morning. After Raqqa had fallen in the hands of its new rulers, his wife and kids fled to Damascus. After a while no one was allowed to leave the Capital of the Caliphate except for a medical emergency—and for one week only.

He managed to get a medical excuse from a doctor who preferred to stay under national and international bombardment so that the new rulers wouldn't confiscate his clinic and house, both of which he had bought with the toil of a lifetime. Thanks to countless checkpoints, the trip to Damascus took two full days instead of seven hours. When he reached his displaced family at night, he found them without water, electricity, cooking gas, or diesel for heating. They were spending their days and nights under covers to warm each other with their bodies.

Two days before his leave of absence expired, he had sneaked out of the covers and returned to distant Raqqa, crestfallen and empty-hearted. As soon as he got home, he sneaked into his empty bed, which he found as cold as frost. His every limb began shivering from the severe cold. Suddenly an overwhelming heat wave engulfed him, melted the frost in his body, and transported him to another world. The dusk visitor—an explosive barrel—has just been sent to warm him and keep him company. It landed, gave him a tight hug, and sucked him with it into the bowels of the earth.

Livestream

Truth TV interrupted its regular transmission shortly before midnight and on came its oldest anchor Nazeera Battah, known among her detractors as Two-Pronged Tongue, to read the following Breaking News:

> In these difficult circumstances when our country is beset by forces of global evil because of the continued struggle of its wise leadership and its steadfast adherence to our national causes, especially the question of Palestine, the fearless leader of our country—the vigilant captain of our ship and our hope of salvation—appoints Dr Taher Abdalla head of the National Committee on Human Rights.

> With a doctorate in law from the Sorbonne and a number of books on human rights in Arabic, French, and English to his name, Dr Abdalla has been a professor at the University of Geneva for a number of years. He has also recently worked for the United Nations High Committee for Human Rights. Dr Taher Abdalla joins us via Skype from Geneva, and we are honored to have him with us.

"Dr Taher Abdalla, welcome to Truth TV."

"Thank you, Nazeera."

"How does it feel to be appointed by the leader of our country as head of the National Committee on Human Rights? And what are your future plans to confront the smear campaign facing our country abroad about allegations of human rights violations?"

"Let me take this opportunity to speak from the heart to your viewers on your so-called Truth TV. It gives me no honor whatsoever to work under the command of a war criminal who destroyed his own country, displaced his own people, and lured foreign invaders and occupiers into. . ."

"We apologize, dear viewers, for this technical error that interrupted our live chat with our guest. But rest assured we will fix things, and fix them good before we return."

And return Nazeera did—a few minutes later. Grumpy and furious, she was like a prowling lioness who spied a prey. She cleared her throat before she started shelling and spewing her improvisations:

> Our viewers around the globe, honored citizens, and valiant people, you have just witnessed a specimen misguided citizen who sold himself to the devil for a handful of dollars in order to stab his country in the back—this same country that had nurtured and educated him at no charge in its national schools and universities, the country that fed him of the bounties of its good earth and air, the country in whose paths, plains, mountains, and valleys he had strolled, the country that turned a deaf ear to the sexual harassment accusations recently pressed against this evil liar by several UN staff members, the country that had turned a blind eye to his disgraceful past when he was convicted of sodomy during his military service with a fellow conscript. Oh how true is the old saying, "A crooked dog tail can never be made straight!" Nay, Allah said it best in His Holy Book, "Such are the Signs of Allah, which We rehearse to thee in truth: then in what exposition will they believe after rejecting Allah and His Signs?" Truth on Truth TV, dear viewers, will enlighten you.

At the Last Checkpoint

A T THE LAST CHECKPOINT, a paratrooper in military fatigues and Adidas shoes examined the driver's face and told him to get off the bus. Scared, the driver asked, "Sir, what's my charge? What have I done wrong? I am just a simple bus driver."

"I just don't like your face."

The passengers held their breath and hoped that this, too, would pass and they would eventually get to their destination in spite of the unexpected delays.

The paratrooper asked the scared driver, "Who's your god, you shithead?"

"He is mine and yours, Sir. I worship the same God as you do, Sir."

"Then let this god of yours save you from me."

He then ordered the bus driver to face a nearby wall. The sun was dazzling. With all his might he assaulted the driver with the butt of his AK47. The assault was so violent that the assailant tripped and accidentally pulled the trigger and killed himself.

The driver and his passengers resumed their much interrupted journey.

IV
THE REPUBLIC OF NAMMOURISTAN

Fourteen longer and more somber stories

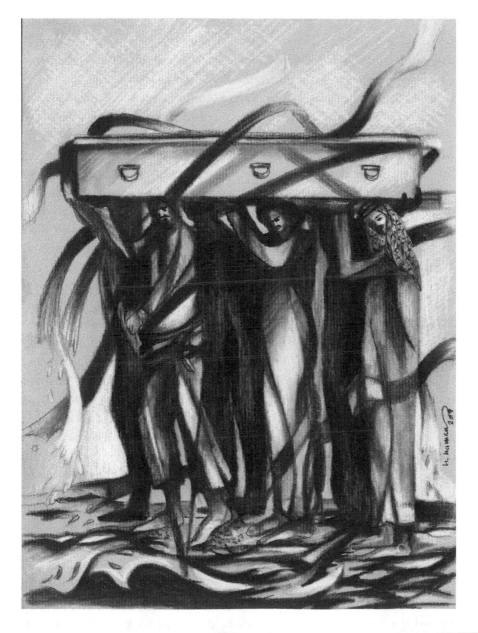

The Swirl

An Account of a Good-for-Nothing Thug

YESTERDAY I CAUGHT MYSELF remembering a distant day from my childhood and discovered, to my shame, that on that day I was a *shabbeeh* (a thug). It is true that *shabbeeh* was not known then as it is nowadays, but what I had done then was indisputably the deed of a *shabbeeh*. And this, mind you, was the only time in my short career of thuggery where I surprised even myself. However, I took only one step in that career and then gave it up, owing to an incorrigible weakness in my personality. And it was this weakness which made me vulnerable in various stages of my life and brought me to my current position: a mere teacher of English poetry, earning his living in exile, while others, with a single panegyric poem, rose to the highest echelons of government, and did not have to leave the country except for vacation or recreation—and at the state's expense, to boot. The disparity between their fortunes and mine was a point my fellow villagers used to shame me on and a reason to call me, every now and then, *khayes*, ie a loser.

But what can I do with my God-given weakness? For instance, when I was little I used to cry whenever my father, may he rest in peace, sang one of his harvest songs while threshing our granary every summer. By nature fond of Bedouin poetry, father used to recite verses by Nimr Ibn Adwan, Rakan Ibn Hithlain, or Abdalla Al-Fadhil Al-Milhim who, upon contracting smallpox, was deserted by his own clan, though he was its chief, which fled to Makhool in the Syrian desert. What grieved me the most was the verses he composed when he woke up from a coma and found that his clan had left him nothing but a deep scar in the heart, a dog named Sheer, and a slaughtered camel, the latter to bribe the dog in order not to desert his companion to beasts of the wilds. Father used to find comfort in the verses of these bards, but they moved me to tears against my will. Or sometimes I would weep loudly, hoping he would stop torturing me, and when I wept I was made the laughing stock of my elder brothers.

I remember one day when I brought my father a tea kettle and some food. When I reached the edge of the threshing floor, I put down the kettle and the food bag on the ground, took off my shoes (because father had taught us that it was sinful to tread upon God's bounty with our shoes), and jumped behind the horse-drawn thresher and held unto its back wooden bumper.

While traipsing clockwise on the threshing floor, I watched with amazement how the thresher's two parallel wooden cylinders, fitted with serrated metal discs, and serving also as wheels, were hungrily grabbing the fresh sheaves of wheat my father was feeding them with a long-handled fork from the top of the granary or briskly throwing them behind the thresher on whose top he was securely perched. My father was singing, as usual, and I think he did not mean to dismount the thresher to eat until he was through with his sad chant. Suddenly, I felt a stinging pain pierce my big left toe, and I screamed at the top of my lungs. My father, lost in his sad chant, went on intoning, "Oh, for a cup of coffee sipped in tranquility . . ." He was totally oblivious to my weeping, thinking perhaps that it was just one more of my seasonal scandals. He didn't realize it was serious until the horse finished a full circle and stood still when he saw me lying in front of him on the threshing floor, flailing and begging him with my clumsy little hand not to trample me under his hooves. I was too paralyzed by pain to move out of his way, and my greatest fear was that he would tear my thin body to pieces if he, along with the thresher and my father, who was drunk on his own dirge, were to pass over me. But by the grace of God, the horse, too unsullied by human lyrics to forget his nature, was quicker than my father in perceiving the catastrophe that was about to befall me. My father, God forgive him, jumped off the thresher and carried me away from the threshing floor. He eased my head on his food bag and started to look for the source of pain. He found a black scorpion, still clinging to my big toe. He said it had died after injecting its entire poison in me, that its stinger was not broken, as would be expected, because my flesh was too tender.

My father tore a strip of his *thobe* and bandaged my toe to stop the poison from spreading to the rest of my body. Then he carried me home in tears. There was no doctor in our village, and the only bus that goes to the city once a day has just come back. So he had to do something. He took out a new Nacet blade and asked mother to close my eyes. He gently started slitting my swollen toe to ooze out the poison and the dark clotted blood. When he has squeezed my toe and the congestion eased, he bent over my big toe and started sucking it. This was the only way he could suck the poison out of my toe. Father's lips were cracked, and by sucking my poisoned toe he was also exposing himself to danger. So he asked mother to bring him the milk pot, from which he started scooping and rinsing the poison out of his mouth. Then he gulped down two or three glasses of milk, just to be on the safe side. Mother made me a malt paste which she bandaged around my whole foot.

All night long, she and father kept comforting me by tears and prayers. God cured me of that sting, but my flesh remained tender, tempting scorpions of another sort to sting it.

When I entered school at the end of that summer, more than forty years ago, father wanted me to excel in it, and I did. But this excellence was cause for both trouble and respect at the same time. Sometimes, older and bigger boys bullied me, but at the same time, I earned the respect of the teachers and the principal of the school. And this was enough of a deterrent to some bullies, at least within the school premises. But outside that, I had no relief but God's mercy and my nimble feet. None of the bullies could catch up with or outrace me, thanks to my agile, lean body. When I instinctively realized that the leanness of my body was a grace from God, I was keen, from an early age, to stay lean in order not to be exhausted by running and be overrun by the fat ones.

I moved on to second grade with excellent marks, especially in spelling and penmanship, despite my tender years. In recognition of this excellence, my teacher has decided to appoint me head of my class right from the first week. But I soon realized that I was not fit for this position because it put me in direct confrontation with the bigger boys who deliberately provoked me and defied my authority. I begged him to relieve me of this honor and he refused. When things got worse, I told my father. He went to the school and spoke with the teacher and begged him to appoint a better suited pupil for the job. I heard the teacher arguing with my father about the necessity of "boosting the pupil's leadership potential" (which I didn't understand then), but my father was adamant and I was relieved of that honor. The teacher, however, remained proud of me, and during recess he would invite me to the teachers' room or the principal's office and ask his colleagues to dictate me whatever passages they liked, and I would write them without mistakes, though I did not understand most of their words.

About two months after the start of the school year, a new teacher from one of the big, distant cities arrived at our rural elementary school. There was no vacancy for this new comer, but he was appointed instead of the sixth grade teacher. The sixth grade teacher was the most senior of the school's staff and the only teacher from our village, but now he was demoted to a comfortable but useless rank. He was made the school librarian, even though our school had no library. One week later, this new comer had apparently heard from my teacher about my talent in spelling and penmanship, and wagered with the principal about something I knew nothing about until Sabri, the school's water-carrier, came to our classroom carrying a summons from the principal.

I accompanied the water carrier, not knowing why I was summoned. In the principal's office, I found the new teacher, though classes had started about fifteen minutes earlier, and all other teachers were in their classes.

Sabri was a distant relative of my mother, and the naughty boys in the school insisted that he was my uncle. This, of course, was simply a convenient shaming device, he being a dwarf. The more I protested, the more the naughty boys and bullies insisted that he was my uncle, who held a disgraceful job as well, and that, try as I might renounce any affinity with this *mashrook*, I was his nephew. *"Mashrook"* means a devil disguised in human form. It was the habit of our village to give each one of its residents a nasty nickname and worked so hard to disseminate it among the people until the original name was forgotten. And because Sabri was the only dwarf in our village, its people, including his own younger brother, wanted to mark his distinction with two nicknames: the first is Mashrook, the second is Soussi, or chick.

Sabri, my hopelessly undeniable "uncle," used to carry water in goatskins from the Euphrates on the back of his donkey two or three times a day. If pupils happened to come out for recess at the same time he was emptying his water skins into the barrel, placed in one corner of the schoolyard, he would lick them so hard with his bamboo cane in order to vent out his anger on their skins before he emptied his load into the barrel. What led him to this practice was this: one day, he was coming back with his third and last load of water for that day, when a huge sixth grader approached and held the donkey's neck for him, while he went to the back of the donkey in order to lift the water skins and slide them down the donkey's haunches. When the two skins almost touched the ground, the naughty fat boy produced a little trumpet and shrieked into the ear of the donkey. Losing his asinine wits, the donkey gave Sabri such a hard kick on the chest that threw him off the ground. And the water was spilled all over the parched schoolyard.

And since then, nothing matched Sabri's thirst for vindictiveness except our desperate desire to quench the thirst in our little throats, now parched from reciting national songs and slogan leaflets periodically distributed to us since the arrival of the new comer to our school. Sabri's bamboo cane gave no consideration to bonds of blood. My share of its kindness was the same as any other pupil whose ill luck put him under its mercy. Sabri neither gave me relief when I was chased by the bullies outside the school premises nor did he ever carry me on the back of his donkey when I labored under the heavy weight of the school bag during the months of scorching heat. Yet, despite all this, in the eyes of the school he was my indisputable *mashrook* uncle.

"You're Salih?" the new comer asked me.

"Yes."

"Go with your uncle to sixth grade."

Uncle? Even you know that Sabri, the *mashrook* water carrier, is my uncle?

When Sabri and I headed towards the sixth grade classroom, the head of the class saw us approaching, and rushing towards the door, he yelled at his charges, "Atteeen-tion! Staaand up!"

The rascals scrambled to their feet, laughing. The chief rascal swung towards us in a deliberately ludicrous manner and raised his right hand, military style, in salute to the two comers.

"The platoon of vanguards," he roared, "is ready for inspection, Sir Soussi, the Mashrook!"

This was a new language we didn't know two months ago. I stood outside the door, stunned. The *mashrook* ran back to bring his bamboo cane and teach these rascals a lesson they won't forget easily. But the teacher came to his class and saved his rascals from a painful vengeance. He sat me in one of the front desks, and from the inside pocket of his jacket he pulled out a roll of papers (later on I learned that it was called a newspaper), opened it on a particular page, and ordered everyone, including me, to be ready for dictation. I borrowed a piece of paper from my neighbor and started writing what the teacher dictated. From the dictated passage I still remember some phrases speaking about our wise leadership and its brave stand against all the machinations of world imperialism, which are designed to undermine the steadfastness of our people to divert our attention away from our sacred cause, the central Arab cause, the cause of usurped Palestine. Actually what helped me remember bits of this passage was the fact that for thirty years after that incident I heard the same phrases tirelessly repeated on our national radio or read them also in our newspapers.

The teacher corrected our test papers on the spot, and only three pupils—I was one of them—scored a full mark. The teacher's face was flushed with anger, and he was booming and fuming, "The disaster does not simply lie in your spelling mistakes; it lies in the fact that in such mistakes you are also committing a wrong against your own country and leader. Let me tell you that what you have just committed is a national treason for which you deserve the severest punishment. Aren't you ashamed that this Salih, a second-grader, and a mere nephew of a *mashrook*, knows how to spell better than you, sixth-graders?" Though the teacher exempted me, in principle, from the serious charge, in reality I couldn't help seeing myself lumped with my fellow traitors, and that I was one of them, willy-nilly. But the feeling of disorientation that classed me, temporarily, with the pack of traitors didn't last long, for the teacher barked at me, "Salih, go to your uncle and get me his bamboo cane!"

My uncle? Even you, traitor catcher!

My "uncle" was more than happy to oblige. In fact, his delight was many times greater in magnitude than his dwarfish size. When I delivered the cane to the teacher, I was surprised to hear him tell me to hold it. Then he ordered the two other pupils, the ones exempted from the charge of high treason, to come out, and he stood them next to the pucker-faced blackboard, on which you can't write a sentence of five words without being interrupted by a hole here and a dent there. The teacher ordered the pack of traitors to hold out their hands and receive a light punishment, this time. Then he turned towards me and ordered me to inflict the decided punishment on those vagabonds.

"Why me, Sir?"

"No objection to a command before carrying it out, Salih!"

I didn't understand what he meant, so I asked him to explain, which he did in terms suitable to my childish capabilities. When I grew up I learned that what he had said was a military expression, nay, one of the staples of military life.

I had no choice but to carry out what I was commanded. So I said, "In the Name of God, the Most Compassionate, the Most Merciful." The teacher laughed at my hillbilly naïveté. I started licking the roguish traitors with my uncle's cane, and I felt particularly triumphant and delighted when I licked two who have always bullied me. When I finished licking the first batch of traitors occupying the front desks of the third and second rows to the left of the door, I headed towards the front desk of the first row to give its occupants whatever punishment I pleased. I was surprised, however, to find none in it but Qasim, or Awjan as our village called him. This Qasim was deformed in all four limbs. Each of his palms was cleft from the ray of the hand between the middle and ring fingers down to the wrist bone. His inwardly curved fingers were extremely white and slender. His feet were also twisted around so that his toes pointed backwards while his heels were up front, unlike ours, us normal people.

Qasim was older than his classmates, which explains why he had a tentative, thin mustache that broke the monotony of his extremely white face. His ears were bigger than any human ears I have ever seen in our village. His father and mine were close friends and neighbors in the fields. But I was a subordinate and had to carry out the instructions of our teacher, and because he was a new guest in our village we had a duty to entertain him. Qasim, who always sat in the first desk after the door because of his disability, was not holding out his hands like the rest of the traitors. When I approached to beat him on his hands, he gave me that disarming look of incredulous surprise and reproof. For a few seconds, we stood facing each other speechlessly. Two reproachful tears fell from his eyes, and words rose in my throat and chocked. I felt all the powers I have just acquired crumbling before his weakness. I rushed out of the classroom towards the open gate of the school. I slipped the bamboo cane under the ruins on the right of the gate from the outside and continued running home. When I felt certain that no runner from the school was after me, I started dragging my feet leisurely. On the way I met one of the dignitaries of our clan who asked me why I was coming back from school so early. I gave him an edited report of what had happened, and he shook his head in disapproval of my voluntary abandonment of a convenient opportunity. Then he spat at me and said, *"khayes!"*

The Swirl

IN THE VILLAGES ON THE NORTHERN BANKS of the Euphrates, *eidul-fitr* festivities end roughly around midday of the first of the three prescribed days. Rarely does a villager take a two-day holiday, for his crops and livestock do not recognize human customs, and the welfare of the villagers—or rather their very survival—depends on recognizing the rights of their domestic flora and fauna to irrigation and grazing, especially in spring and summer. As for *eidul-adhha*, well, it remains in effect until the last heifer is sacrificed in the afternoon of the first day. The reason for waiting until the afternoon to conclude the festivities is that our village had only one unprofessional butcher: the imam of our mosque. And slaughtering, skinning, and quartering her takes a lot of time, and the imam wouldn't allow anyone else to slaughter sacrificial heifers. Also, there are times when the heifer escapes from her butchers, and it takes a considerable amount of time to catch and drag her back to her inevitable fate.

Though our village did not raise cows, whoever wanted to sacrifice one on behalf of his late mother or father had to go before *eidul-adhha* to the city of Deir Ezzoar or the surrounding villages and bring back a red heifer, a sight to see, a feast to the eyes. No one sacrificed a sheep, a goat, or even a ram, for that was considered a shameful attempt to stint his father or mother, patiently waiting in their graves, their dues. The deceased may wait for years and years before a son fulfilled his duties, either because of lack of means, negligence, or sheer filial impiety. In this latter case, the dead would have to appear to his son in a dream and chide him, explicitly or implicitly. To be visited by the dead in a dream is far more terrible than being served a subpoena by the local police summoning him to appear in the criminal court in the city about a charge he knows nothing about. That's why some of the well-to-do tended to sacrifice for themselves while still alive, during their last days when they were more preoccupied by thoughts of death than by thoughts of life.

During *eidul-adhha*, children's joy peaked in the cemetery when the living visited their dead at daybreak and threw charity candies over their graves, and children rushed and jostled each other to collect as much as they could. When pockets were filled with the harvest of the graveyard, the older children went back to the village and doled it out to their sleeping brothers and sisters.

Father, God bless his soul, was a strangely disposed man. Unlike many villagers, he wouldn't allow us to visit the cemetery for the sole purpose of collecting candies. Nor would he take anyone of us to a *fatiha* recitation at the house of another villager. A *fatiha* recitation is an invitation to dinner, after which the guests and their host recite the *fatiha,* the opening *sura* of the Quran, to the repose of a recently dead person's soul. *Fatiha* recitations are observed as long as the death of the loved one hurts the bereaved, and are usually held once or twice a year. Very often, the ritual is suspended after the third year, even among the well-to-do. Father also wouldn't allow mother, may she rest in peace as well, to use vegetable oil in cooking, nor to raise goats or chickens. To him, these things were ungentlemanly pursuits. When my sister Fatma wanted to buy a sewing machine—a Singer—he was mortified by the idea of her taking up a disgraceful industry, though she was married and had a whole brood of children, and she only wanted to sew clothes for them. But he relented when she, his firstborn and dearest child whom he had named after his late mother, begged him. Though he was proud of his chosen paedonymic, Abu Sayel, if he got angry with Sayel, he would snap, "To hell with Sayel, I'm Abu Fatma!" He was also proud of his German rifle, his horse, and his small herd of sheep.

But when my young paternal uncle Hammoud died of a stroke, and my cousin Ahmad was killed in the War of Attrition with Israel in 1974, he allowed us to visit the cemetery on religious holidays. We kept this up for four years. Then one day my brother Naji, whose name means 'survivor,' decided to stop going to the cemetery. He was now a young man of seventeen, and it was inappropriate for him to go for candies. On the eve of *eidul-adhha* I asked him reproachfully, "Don't you want to recite the *fatiha* for your uncle and cousin?" He said, "I don't need to go to the graveyard to recite the *fatiha*. I will recite it from here, on *eids* and other occasions." Then he raised his hands towards heaven, and his lips began moving silently. When he stroked his face with his hands, signaling that he finished his recitation, I was certain that I would miss my share of the graveyard harvest this *eid.*

On the morning of *eidul-adhha,* we woke up later than usual. We exchanged *eid* greetings with family and relatives, and ate the sweets my father had bought for this occasion and stowed away from us in order not to eat them before the due time. To our surprise, he had also slaughtered a fat lamb for this occasion, and also because my brother Sayel has recently been employed in the Euphrates Basin Project in Raqqa after his graduation from the Agricultural High School in Deir Ezzoar. My brother was one of the first boys in the village who graduated from high school and found a job in the city. Father's joy was indescribable when Sayel stood surety for him in an agricultural water pumps dealership. The old Blackstone motor pump was frequently out of order, and failed him in the very middle of the season. It refused to respond to all attempts at resuscitation by the *mécaniques* of Raqqa. In a fit of anger, he dumped it in the Euphrates and swore by divorce that he would buy a brand new Polish Andoria pump even if he had to sell all of his sheep.

After we had eaten our fill and had our tea, father abruptly announced the end of *eid* for me and my brother Naji. He ordered us to ride the horse and go irrigate the *haweeja* cotton field.

"In this scorching summer and on the first day of *eidul-adhha*, father?"

"Yes, because it is scorching, the horse needs to drink, and what is left of *haweeja* needs irrigation, otherwise the cotton flowers will wither and die. And if they do, we'll be empty handed at the end of the season."

We knew that it was pointless to argue with our father, but we tried anyway, and the result was as expected. Reluctantly we rode the horse, who was the happiest of the three. About twenty minutes later, we reached the *haweeja*, overlooking a steep cliff on the northern bank of the Euphrates. We took the horse to the river, and he drank until he had his fill. Then he sighed gratefully, as if to say, "Thank you, Uncle Abu Sayel, and Happy Eid to you!" We left him to graze in a grassy stretch between the edge of the water and the cliff beyond which our semi-sandy land stretched for hundreds of meters. Our *haweeja* was originally an island in the middle of the river (hence the local name *haweeja)*, and when the water level used to recede from springtime onwards, our folks crossed over and sowed the *haweeja* with seeds of string beans and watermelon. Come harvesting time, they would cross back and forth to pick the fruits of their labor. But after Turkey had constructed a number of dams, and Syria built the Great Euphrates Dam, the water level dropped so severely that the width of the river course was reduced from thousands to hundreds of yards. This resulted in the birth of huge swathes of land on both sides of the river, which were exploited and reclaimed by rural pioneers, even though the new lands were mostly uncultivable either because they were too sandy or too pebbly.

We entered the canopy in which our green Polish Andoria was sitting solemnly, covered by the red rug we always threw on it every evening to protect it from sandstorms. Our piece of land was unleveled and square in shape, bordered on the north by a sand dune offsetting it from the land of our eldest uncle. Right in its middle, there was one big canal. When this canal reached the northern border it branched off into two smaller canals: one going east to irrigate the eastern rectangle; the other going west to irrigate the opposite rectangle. Each rectangle had four rows of beds, sloping from north to south, while between each two rows of beds there was another branch canal to serve them. We used to start irrigating from the farthest and highest point down to the edge of the cliff. When we finished irrigating the farthest row of beds, we would channel the water to the next row, and so on and so forth until we irrigated the row next to the mother canal. When all eight rows were thus irrigated, we would have completed one cycle, and a week later we would start all over again until harvesting time.

I haven't yet come of age, agriculturally speaking. So my job was limited to keeping an eye on the mother and branch canals, watching the beds from outside, making tea, and occasionally visiting the motor pump just in case it was hungry for more oil or diesel.

Before the *eid,* only the western rectangle, to the left of the mother canal, was left un-irrigated. It was also the hardest, for its upper terraced beds were the steepest, smallest, and fastest to irrigate; while its lower beds, lying directly above the edge of the cliff, were level and bigger in size. The irrigation of the cliff beds has its own rituals that none can tell you about like an expert. One such ritual is that a farmer wishing to drink a glass of tea, or grab a quick miserable morsel, or smoke a cigarette has to wait until it is time to irrigate these beds.

The closer to the cliff, the more clayey the sandy soil got, and this gave the soil a stickier texture and as such was more cultivable. These beds were also infested with rats which dug holes from the surface of beds down to the upper strata of the cliff, thus causing irrigation water to leak out, and may even lead to the collapse of part of the cliff whose lower strata had many caves and vaults to which jackals flocked at night after their raids on watermelons and other edible fruits. No tractor ever ventured to plow these cliff beds lest the cliff collapses under its heavy weight. That's why we made do with cultivating them with traditional primitive means.

The leakage of water from the surface of the bed to the upper strata of the cliff is known as *ghuwwala,* ie swirl. That is why whenever we came to the last bed, we inspected it for rat holes. If we found any, we filled them with earth to stoppage them. Then one of us would stand above the edge of the cliff to watch for any leakage, while the other kept an eye for any swirl signs in the water-filling bed. If the swirl was detected before the bed was filled with water, it would be easy to stoppage the rat hole. But if the bed was nearly filled to the brim, and you suddenly saw a little eddy developing in the middle of the bed, you had better channel the water to another bed and stay away until the water was completed drained; otherwise, you might be sucked by the water pressure into the gorge that has opened up into the belly of the cliff. Yet, despite all these precautionary measures, we were not always lucky to find these treacherous rat holes, whose upper vents might sometimes be simply unsuspicious little cracks in the clayey bed.

We cranked the motor pump, and started irrigating the farthest row of beds from the top down to the bottom bed at the cliff edge. Things went fine, and we forgot the bitterness we had felt after being forced by our father to cut our *eid* short. Our horse was also grazing on lush green grass below the cliff, the cotton tree leaves were getting brighter and brighter, what with their roots being saturated, and the temperature beginning to drop in the late afternoon. The rising breezes of the Euphrates refreshed our bodies, already relishing the feel of mud and water. When we got to the last bed, Naji asked me to keep an eye on the cliff, while he was in the middle of the bed on the lookout for any swirl to nip it in the bud. The bed was rather spacious, the land parched, and it would take a long time for the cotton bed to fill up with water and the thirst of its trees quenched. When there was no leakage from the side of the cliff and no swirl from the bed above, Naji asked me, "How about a cup of tea?" I went to gather dry driftwood and look for three clumps of hard clay to serve as tripods for the kettle. Then I went to the canopy and brought the tea kit. I descended the cliff and waded about two meters into the river water. Bending my back, I held my right arm as far as possible and scooped a kettleful of clean water. I came back and set the driftwood ablaze. In a few minutes, the water was boiling. I dumped two glassfuls of sugar into the boiling kettle—farmers like their tea very sweet. Waiting until the sugar melted, I scooped a bit of loose tea and dumped it into the kettle. When I figured that my thick sweet syrup was ready, I invited my brother to have a glass. But he was too busy uprooting alfa weeds, now becoming easy after their roots have been flooded with water. I called him again, but he ignored me and went on uprooting alfas. Holding the handle of the shovel with his left hand and uprooting the alfas with his right, he was stooping and slowly moving towards me. The water was rising in the bed and nearing capacity. Close to the edge of the bed, he found a small licorice plant and he had a fancy to uproot it as well. I told him to leave it alone because licorice plants have very deep roots going here and there for several meters. But he didn't listen to my advice—perhaps because I was too young to be considered agriculturally knowledgeable.

He drove the shovel deep into the water-saturated earth, then squatted in the water to scoop the mud from around the root of the plant with his hands. When he was certain he could uproot it, he stood above it, putting his feet into the pit he has just scooped out, and jerked it strongly. From the bowels of the earth, about a meter-long root slithered into his hands. With the strong jerk and the unexpected compliance of the root, my brother fell on his back. All of a sudden, a horrifying deep chasm was opened up under him and he was quickly swept off by the roaring water. I only heard his gasp when he was buried under the landslide. There was none around I could call for help and I knew that exhuming him was beyond my ability, and there was also the risk of being personally swept off by the landslide. I rode the horse and raced the wind. In a few minutes I was in the village. I was tongue-tied, so I used sobs and signs to tell my father and his companions that a catastrophe had befallen my brother. The entire village rushed to the river bank, on foot and mounted, grabbing whatever axes, shovels, and other tools they found within quick reach.

In the midst of tragedy, I had forgotten to turn off the Andoria, and when the rescuers came running, we heard from afar its sad sunset tunes echoed by the cliff, together forming a ceremonious Euphrates orchestra playing a requiem for the prematurely departed. When we came to the *haweeja,* no one needed me to point out the scene of the tragedy. The *ghuwwala's* troubled water, rushing from the cliff to the river, was visible from a distance. During my absence, the water had cut a deep ravine into the sandy cliff. My brother's corpse was exhumed by now, the muddy water galloping around it. The first one to reach it said that he saw a jackal roaming around the place before help arrived.

Mother wanted to throw herself into the river, but some women held her, reminding her that this was God's will. She returned with the mourners, lamenting and beating her face until we arrived home. The following morning, they carried my brother to the graveyard, the women mourners raised a loud lament, and my sister Fatma stepped forward to lead the choir of keeners.

Never before has my sister participated in keening or chanted lamentation chants, but it seemed that the death of her beloved brother stirred up the latent seeds of creativity in her soul. Other women keeners gathered around her, and they all took to beating their chests and cheeks in perfectly synchro-nized rhythms with the sad chants she was improvising. I had expected my father to get his German rifle and fire a full magazine, as he had done a few years ago when they carried his younger brother Hammoud to his final abode, or when the Squad of Military Ceremonies lowered the coffin of his nephew in his grave then fired twenty one rounds in salute to the martyr. But he was silent and speechless. The procession of mourners marched and I marched part of the way with them. Suddenly, I decided to go back home and be alone. When the mourners came back from the graveyard, one of them asked me reproachfully, "How come you lagged behind and didn't attend your brother's burial?" "You are the ones who lagged behind," I said to him. "I was the first one to witness his burial yesterday afternoon!" Then I raised both hands towards heaven and recited the *fatiha* for my brother, uncle, and martyred cousin.

Our Father
Who Art in the Vatican

THERE WAS NO TALKING HIM OUT OF IT. He was truly a master at the game of persistence. He wanted my address and requested the honor of visiting me at home—a visit that, he hoped, would be followed by many mutual visits in the future. I sought refuge in God and resigned myself completely to His own dispensation.

I had then just moved out of an apartment in a dilapidated building to another where at least the new building had sturdier walls and the residents were more interactive with the latest hits, whether new or traditional folk songs recast in modernist garb. In the new building, Shahrazad, our neighbor's daughter, and her younger sisters took to serenading us every night from one thirty past midnight to three thirty in the morning, playing "I, the Brunette Reaper" by Ali Al-Deek (Ali the Cock) over and over again. The dancing heels reeled so feverishly over my head that I felt they were about to bore through the concrete ceiling that concealed our primeval nakedness and precluded our soldering together in a bacchanalia of tantalizing rapture and torment. Helpless, I would pronounce two or three curses every night against our terrorist neighbors who reminded me of our cousins in Guantanamo. But there was no stopping the Cock's blaring undulations before the morning crows announced daybreak. It was only then that the dancing bodies relaxed and the heels stopped reeling; it was only then that the playful Shahrazad was quiet and ready to sleep.

***

"Hello. Yes. Who?"

"Don't you recognize my voice? I am Mr. Abu Nabigha."

"Nabigha of Thubyan?"

"Thank you for the flattering joke, Professor. I am not that much of a poetic genius, you know. Where are you?"

"We've just left Tartous."

"So, you will arrive in Lattakia after sunset?"

"God willing."

"I request the honor of meeting you. Sir, I am burning to meet you."

"Well, I'm burning to get back to my wife. I have left her at dawn going to Damascus."

"I know; I've called her several times to get your cellphone number. Where's your home? I'd like to come and say congratulations."

"Listen, Sir. I am exhausted. I slept only one hour last night. I traveled seven-hundreds kilometers to and fro in this sweltering heat, and you insist on meeting me tonight?"

"Yes, you have no way out of this."

"Then, let that be in the Suez Café."

"The Suez Café?"

"At nine sharp. You will recognize me by my dirty shirt."

In the Suez Café he was waiting for me like a desperate farmer who took his cow to be inseminated by a bull in the next village. Hoary head, drooping lower lip, dusty face. I thought he was just pulled out of the rubble or inundated by a Mediterranean Tsunami. The café was bustling with its daily run of customers: intellectuals, penniless aficionados, neo-revolutionaries, and simple folk who punctuated every drag on their hubble-bubbles with a philosophic truism or two in unsullied Slayba dialect.

"Well, I didn't expect you to be this young, Professor."

"I hope you have no problem with that."

"On the contrary. That makes me admire you even more. But it is strange that our Comrade, the Party Branch Secretary, doesn't know you."

"Why should that be strange? I never knocked at his door to beg him for a post or to submit a report about a colleague. By God, I don't even know where his office is located."

"But you work at the same university and he is your boss."

"Listen here, Mister. He may be the boss of people like you, but he can never be my boss."

"I meant no offense, Professor. Please forgive me. I'm only like a big brother to you."

"I have no doubt whatsoever that you wish to give me the treatment of a big brother."

From a leather case he produced a folded piece of paper wrapped with a purple lace. He unwrapped it, and then slipped it in my hand. He asked me to do him the honor of reading it. I took the piece of paper and began reading it silently.

"I want to hear it in your own fine poetic voice that so many told me about."

"But it is your own poem, and I haven't even read it yet. At least, give me the chance to read it once."

He did so after he saw that I was blasé to his importunities.

"As you can see, it is an occasional poem. I wrote it on the occasion of the recent visit by His Holiness Pope John Paul II to the country. My cousin, the Governor, secured for me a meeting with His Holiness and I read it in His presence. It won the admiration of His Holiness for it paid tribute to His noble stance towards every just cause of ours. The poem also highlighted the fact that our country was the cradle of Christianity and the bridge on which it crossed to Europe."

"But you said nothing His Holiness does not know already!"

"But I said that in verse."

"True, and no one seems to have given the devil his due. Now, tell me: since when have you been smitten with the germ of versification."

"Well, to tell you the truth, this is my first poem. But to tell you another truth, our village is full of poets. There is a poet in every house. I have spent many years of my life teaching the village boys in the morning and farming in the afternoon. Frankly speaking, I wrote the poem with encouragement from one of my former pupils, a gifted poet, mind you, who now works for the Ministry of Tourism. Lo and behold! the Pope gave me a precious brass icon as a reward for that sisterless poem of mine. I hung it up in the entrance of my humble home, which you will see when you do us the honor of visiting us."

He bent his head over the small table between us and beckoned that I should do the same as if he wanted to divulge a dangerous secret, "By the way, our comrade, the Party Branch Secretary, was one of my pupils. But it's been over thirty years or so." He pulled back and so did I.

"What do you want from me?" I asked.

"I want you to translate the poem."

"Just like that? Why? It's an occasional poem that has no sisters yet. It served its purpose by your own admission."

"True, but His Holiness doesn't know Arabic well enough to appreciate the potential beauty of this great language."

"Didn't you yourself admit that it had won His admiration and that He had rewarded you for it?"

"That I did."

"There is no need to translate it, then. Isn't the Pope Catholic?"

"He is, but I don't know what you mean."

"Well, since your poem won the admiration of the greatest shepherd of the Catholic Church in the whole wide world, then that means that it automatically won the admiration of more than a billion of his followers. Man—nay, let me call you Mr. Abu Nabigha—in the realm of poetry you reign supreme.

Do you know that none of Nizar Qabbani's collections sells more than three thousand copies? Whereas you, my Lord, the whole Catholic world stands solidly behind you!"

"Well, thank you very much indeed. By God, I hadn't thought of that."

"Do you know, Sir, that the word 'catholic' in English means 'all-embracing' and 'all- inclusive'?"

"Really?"

"Let Noah Webster be the judge between you and me."

Abu Nabigha was pleased with what my tongue concocted under duress and exhaustion. I even suggested that I would personally write a few lines and send them to the Pope via the Vatican Embassy in Damascus so that His Holiness would know that Abu Nabigha's poem was not an exceptional case written on the spur of the moment. And so I pulled out a piece of paper and I began scribbling some hasty words on it that, I claimed, paid tribute to His revolutionary struggle with all the toiling workers in the world:

> Our father who art in the Vatican,
> Hallowed be thy name.
> We question not thy judgment
> In matters of verse or prose,
> For thou stinteth naught
> To the desperate and exhausted!

A Sojourner Reporting
from Amman

I AM AN ECONOMIC REFUGEE-TURNED-TRAVELER. I chose Amman to be the final destination of my wanderings. I was enchanted by the city's fine buildings, fresh air, fruits and vegetables neatly stacked at the corners of its clean streets. I came to Amman to breathe to the full capacity of my lungs, bury poverty, and substitute the anguish of a love lost in my country with the anguish of another that can never be lost. Amman is a city of smooth stones, but its people seem gruff and grumpy upon first encounter. No sooner do you ask one of them a question than he brusquely answers "What?"—a curt reply that kills in you the desire to repeat a question you know full well that he heard and understood, but this "what?" is a native son's privilege he exercises upon you, the fugitive fleeing from your own country. But then you realize it is more of a conventional verbal reflex than a privilege, because he exercises it without any enduring aggressiveness or superiority. And when you thank him with evident humility, he replies with unexpected kindness, "You're very welcome."

The following day after my arrival in Amman, I met him. I didn't recognize him at first. I only saw a mass of muscles rolling towards me as aggressively and provocatively as a boulder loosened from a mountaintop by torrential downpours. My fears were further increased by the fact that this terrifying mass was wearing black glasses worthy of intelligence agents. I suspected an evil intention, and was about to retract my steps or change my course when he lifted his glasses and gave me that sly, stern grin of his.

"Man, you're scary without these glasses. So why wear them?"

When we embraced, I felt the firm mass of his muscles desperately trying to be released from his tight shirt. Had I not known him well, I would have certainly turned to my heels. His once traditional clothes have given way now to a pair of Versace pants and a sleeveless close-fitting shirt. Even his hair was cut à la Versace. His clothes could hardly contain the volcanic mass of muscles poised to erupt at the slightest provocation. Is it the new style that accentuated a once subdued physique? Can it be possible? What happened to him? Is this really Labeeb Faseeh, the linguist and translator I know? These questions, however, were not articulated by my lips that have been long preoccupied by more absurd questions.

"Yes, I'm your good old friend."

"What brought you to Amman?"

"The same reasons that brought you! A certified Sri Lankan!"

"Wow! I thought you became one of those out-of-sight VIPs of government."

"God forbid! That is the lot of the prosperous and fortunate. What held you so far from joining our caravan of Sri Lankans?"

"Numerous circumstances. But tell me: how long have you been here in Amman? What happened to you?"

"I've been here for the last three years. And I have seen a lot, my friend. As you know, before the last time we met, I was invited for an interview with a deputy minister in our wise government to look at my qualifications in translation. I was then dreaming of a not too expensively priced wife and a decent salary to sustain me, her, and the inevitable brood. I hated, in principle, what our government called the honorable obligation of outsourcing its own qualified cadres to other Arab countries as part of its pan-Arab orientation to wean these countries of their extreme ideological desertification."

"I see that under the volcano of muscles there simmers another volcano."

"Brother, are we human beings or commodities to be loaned? Tell me, why does every one of our consecutive governments behave as if improving the income of its own citizens were the duty of other Arab governments, while improving its own income is our duty? In return for what? Why don't our ministers loan their own children to the rest of the Arab countries in order to wean them of their so-called ideological impoverishment?"

"I thought you had occupied a high position up there, but I see that you're like a powder keg."

"No, that never happened. They called me on the first of April to set the appointment for the fifth of June. I should've known the result beforehand. One of my acquaintances had recommended me to a certain Excellency, and I went on the ominous day, while our newly installed satellite channels were regurgitating, on this historic anniversary, an old song warning our Israeli enemy, 'Woe to you, enemy, woe to you!'"

"Of course. No voice is louder than that of the battle cry."

"As I said, I went on the ominous day. I was sweating and perplexed. I greeted His Excellency, but He ignored it. He kept flipping through a bundle of papers in front of Him, and when He looked up at me with His piercing eyes, I found myself collapsing on the seat His Excellency did not deign to ask me to sit on. And I think He did not forgive me this breach of protocol."

"How did the rest go?"

"He asked me to recite my full name, to name all my paternal and maternal uncles, and mention the clan of my step-mother, bless her soul."

"Perhaps His Excellency was simply mimicking the TV program Who Wants to Be a Millionaire? And as such, His Excellency's initial questions were designed to encourage and warm you up."

"Wait, my friend. His Excellency asked me only one more question that fell on me like a thunderbolt. He asked, 'Are you politically clean or what?' I tried to swallow but couldn't. I tried again and found that my tongue was stiff. I said to myself, 'This is not a question but a trap. A road bump, Labeeb.' I was stunned and disoriented. After some time, I don't know how long it was, I found my bearings and was about to tell him, 'Rest assured, Your Excellency, that I follow neither Osama bin Laden nor Trotsky.'"

"And did you say that?"

"No, I couldn't. I couldn't find my tongue. It had deserted me, I, a man ironically called Labeeb Faseeh, nonetheless. Walked out on me like a jackass which found the gate of the stable open. Add to that, His Excellency's secretary came to inform Him that Mademoiselle Softie, producer of An Official Live, has just arrived. I said to myself, 'My place is like that of Christ among the Jews.' I stood up, while tens of inarticulate sentences and crude thoughts were trapped at the bottom of my throat. The door was opened, a storm of perfume blew in, and, *voila,* Mademoiselle Softie! I stepped back—for, per protocol, it is inappropriate to have your rear end, especially when it is not of the caliber of Mademoiselle Softie's, be the last thing seen by Excellencies. While I was walking backwards unsteadily, Softie's cameraman stepped in, dragging his camera cables behind him. When I estimated that I reached the door, I commissioned my right hand to thank His Excellency on behalf of my still tied tongue. I didn't realize, on my return journey to freedom and poverty, that I had unwittingly stepped on the cables of the camera. The cameraman jerked the cables so violently from under my feet that I fell on my rear end, which the rosy marble floor welcomed with leery lust."

"Ouch! Anyway, I'm glad to see you after all these years. You won't get away from me this time. I know you: You just up and disappear like the seven sleepers of the den."

"No, I won't disappear anymore. But you must excuse me for now because I'm late for my gym, and we'll meet in the evening."

"What's a gym?"

"It's a place where I do weight lifting."

"You? A well-known linguist and translator lifting weights?"

"How did I get these muscles, then?"

"This is the first time I hear that a translator lifts weights! This is hard labor, not an exercise."

"Let me update your outdated knowledge. First of all, I'm known only to a few people like you. And these few people, if you'd excuse my saying, are like dinosaurs in the late Jurassic age. We live outside history. Clinically dead. In our golden age, a caliph used to pay a translator the weight of his translated manuscript in gold. We're about to be extinct, my friend."

"And second of all?"

"And second, my weight lifting stems from my desire to keep up with the pulse of modern life. But first and foremost, it's a practical necessity."

"You speak like a TV channel."

"My friend, I teach here in a private university known to all and sundry for the endless fights among and with its student population. And the fights here are just like our national days there: no sooner do we finish celebrating one than we begin preparing for the next. These fights are of two kinds: fights among the students and are usually instigated by a boy spotting a girl speaking to a young man from an enemy clan or a football match lost the day or night before by a team that has many fans among the students. The second kind of fights is between students and their teachers."

"Shucks, has it come to this?"

"Yes, it has. Of course, the teacher is always the loser, because he is the variable element while the student is the constant one in the university's calculations. And the customer is always right, as stipulated by the Arab market rights list. You're a professor of economics and can understand these terms. And the reasons are manifold, though mostly revolving around a low grade or an exam date that doesn't suit the student's schedule of 'extracurricular' activities."

"But what has all of this to do with your going to . . . What do you call it?"

"I had some experiences, and I realized that I had no relief but from the strength of my arm. It's like the staff of our Lord Moses. I haven't used it so far, and I hope I will never have to."

"Like what?"

"One day, I was giving a lecture around three in the afternoon when I heard a back-and-forth banging in front of the closed door of the classroom. I came out and found two male students, as big as two bison bulls, each standing at one end of the corridor and kicking an empty Pepsi can to the other. The can kept whizzing past me, above me, or between my legs. When it hit me, one of them told me, 'For god's sake, man! Now get back to your classroom and don't fuck around here anymore.'"

"You scare me with this. What did you do?"

"I stopped the lecture and dismissed the students. The following morning, I went to the head of the department and he advised me to stop whining, 'Take it easy, man, take it easy!' Then the same problem happened again and again, and I went to see the dean of the college, who is also the biggest stakeholder in the university. And after a heated and pointless discussion, he said, 'Listen here, Mister. What do you expect me to do? Don't you know these students are from Salt?'"

"What's Salt?"

"A town to the west of Amman whose inhabitants are known for being quarrel mongers."

"Were those students really from Salt?"

"I don't know, but what I know for sure is that the nervous nellies paint the Saltians as if they were above the law, and they are not necessarily so. These cowards think they can scare us with these tactics."

"How was the problem solved?"

"By itself. The school year ended, and I didn't see those bison bulls afterwards. But the next year, something even worse happened to an Iraqi colleague who had fled from Saddam's tyranny and Clinton's smart sanctions."

"Is there worse than you have already told me?"

"Oh, yes. One student beat the hell out of his Iraqi teacher in the university bus depot because he had failed him last semester. So he took revenge at the first chance he had at next commencement. And had it not been for the intervention of magnanimous bus drivers, we would have recited the *fatiha* to the repose of our Iraqi colleague's soul a long time ago."

"What did the university administration do?"

"It duly dismissed the student from the university. But the next day, a delegation of clan chiefs headed to the board of stakeholders and gave them a choice of two bitters: rescind the student's dismissal or all the clan's boys and girls enrolled in the university will be pulled out of it and go to another. And there is no shortage of private universities, you know."

"Oh, come on, man, you're exaggerating. This is pure fiction."

"No, that's reality, my friend, but a magic reality whose various manifestations we live every day at private universities. This is the latest fad of globalization: big fish eat small fish."

"What happened next?"

"Upon the instructions of the board of stakeholders, the Rector was forced to overturn his own decision to dismiss the student. But, truth be told, he issued a new decision to dismiss the professor."

"Good for him! Brother, please take me to this . . . what do you call it?"

"What do you need the gym and body building for? You've just arrived."

"I don't know yet why I need it. But, as we economists say, it is an investment in the future."

Summoned to the Booth

BARELY A FULL DAY BEFORE THE CONVENTION of a symposium on "The Ethics, Research, and Clinical Applications of Stem Cells" at a Saudi university where I worked, I was notified that I had been nominated as one of two interpreters for the day-long proceedings. Certainly, not enough time to do the necessary homework for the job. I was no less daunted when I was further told that four internationally outstanding stem cell researchers from Australia and Saudi Arabia were going to speak, *inter alia,* about the advantages of using stem cells in treating hitherto incurable diseases, while another four scholars were to speak about the Islamic guidelines governing the use of such cells.

As interpreters, our job was to translate a total of eight speeches: four speeches by the four scientists from English into Arabic, and four speeches by the Islamic jurists from Arabic into English. Neither of us had any grounding in either medical science or Islamic jurisdiction—the two fields whose esoteric jargons we were to grapple with the following day with abundant apprehension and uncertain comprehension. And until then I had not met my fellow interpreter who was to be flown in from Riyadh on the morning of the symposium. But it was such a relief to learn that he was a seasoned professional and the personal interpreter for the Saudi Minister of Higher Education. I, on the other hand, had on occasion moonlighted as an informal interpreter, but never served in any remotely "official" capacity except for about thirty minutes in my life, and that was thirteen years ago! And the talks I had to interpret then were far more mundane than the proceedings of this hair-raising event.

Since that sisterless experience, I had gone on to translate various books in the fields of literature, literary criticism, political philosophy, and biography, a few of which were commissioned by reputable publishers or internationally accredited cultural institutions—and I even authored a textbook on literary translation. It was this reputation, alas, that landed me in trouble. In other words, I was suspected of being an interpreter because many people do not readily see the fundamental difference between a translator and an interpreter. While it is my firm belief that every interpreter worthy of his/ her name can also be a competent translator, even competent translators cannot, ipso facto, be all-purpose interpreters, let alone competent ones.

When I expressed doubts about my own adequacy for the job to Dr Adnan Al-Qurashi, the vice-president of the university, he tentatively offered me the chance to turn tail, but before I had the opportunity to take him up on his offer, he tantalizingly quipped, "If you can't do it, who else can?" So I had really no choice but to accept the challenge. To allay my burning anxiety, I suppose, he kindly escorted me to the Grand Auditorium on campus where the symposium was to be held. There, I was introduced to the technical support team who took me to the interpreter's booth, directly below the women's balconied section at the back of the auditorium, and briefly familiarized me with the necessary tools of my newfound trade. I was also given the schedule of events, which included the abstracts of the scientific papers and the bio-data of the speakers. No such luxury, however, was accorded me about the Islamic *illuminati*—except their names and the titles of their papers! So, I was completely in the dark about the substance of their talks, and there was nothing for me to do except wait for not a few, probably unpleasant, surprises the following day.

At home, the uphill trudge began in earnest soon after sunset. I read through the abstracts and CVs once, underlining all the unfamiliar vocabulary items in the process, then I read them again and again with a non-specialized dictionary in hand and tried to find the meanings of those unyielding medical terms. I labored from 6:00 pm to 1:00 am. By then I felt somewhat confident and was ready to crash in the arms of sweet slumber. However, drowsiness could not rout my anxiety until 3:00 am. With just three hours of sleep—by no means enough to keep me mentally and physically alert during the nine-hour speech-a-thon—I, the crestfallen would-be-interpreter, headed to my Golgotha.

Once there, I sought out Dr Al-Qurashi, a well-known pediatric surgeon and the former dean of the college of medicine, for help with terms I could not find in Al-Mawrid Al-Kabeer. Once again, he was helpful and encouraging, though he laughed off the idea of my bringing the fat bilingual tome. In the interpreter's booth, I found my fellow interpreter, a Sudanese, already well-established there. Another chair was brought in for me and we were both sandwiched in the same tight space. The events commenced after some delay and I translated the opening remarks of the rector given in Arabic—and that was an easy kick-off for me, then came the real Armageddon: the first scientific speech given in English by a Monash University stem cell researcher.

Until then I was under the impression that we were to translate consecutively. But as soon as the first speaker began reading his second sentence without waiting for me to finish translating his first, I fathomed the depth of the fix I was in. Moreover, because the symposium did not start on time, speakers in the first session were asked to cut their speeches by ten minutes each. To comply with the moderator's request and their own desire to deliver as much of their prepared speeches as possible, they simply spoke as fast as their speech organs could afford. We the helpless interpreters had neither the authority nor the wherewithal to issue these "violators" any speeding tickets. In addition, there was no real communication between speakers and interpreters. While we could hear the speakers, they could not hear our translation. Moreover, all speakers but one, sounded on our receiving end too soft-spoken that as soon as we began translating, their speech was almost totally drowned by ours. This entailed our omission of significant portions of their papers. No amount of conjecture or improvisation on our part could do to fill up the resulting lacuna. Moments of embarrassed silence, especially in my case, punctuated our panting efforts to cope, too.

In light of the circumstances, only a superhuman genius could simultaneously joggle listening, comprehending, and speaking together. Ordinary mortals, on the other hand, may not be so dexterous.

Much to our chagrin, the scientific speeches were studded with acronyms and other technical punctilios. And there was no shortage of physical bedevilments, either. To stay awake, we had to resort to frequent intakes of caffeine. But the more caffeine we chugged down, the more trips we needed to make to the bathrooms, which were neither close by nor always available— as there were only two at the front of the auditorium. We fought drowsiness and mental attrition with other weapons as well during inter-sessions: splashes of cold water on our faces, short walks outdoors, commiserating, and exchanging jokes. But sleep seems to have a subtle way of knocking down all such paper-thin fortifications. A few minutes after returning to the booth for the first afternoon session, I was plodding at my job as best as I could when lo and behold I heard a loud and clear snore on my right. I had no time to turn but quickly dug my fellow sufferer in the ribs with my elbow, and he dutifully awoke. Like Conrad's French man-of-war, I resumed my hurtling verbal bombardment at an invisible, and by now thinning, audience.

A high point in my day, however, was my completely satisfactory rendition of the last speech in the symposium. The speaker was a Jordanian professor of Islamic studies who spoke about the Islamic guidelines regarding the use of stem cells. I happened to have met him just the day before when I gave him a lift from campus to the city, and we quickly established some cordial rapport. Though he spoke faster than any other speaker in the symposium, I managed to translate nearly all he said with equal speed. But there was something about him that was lacking in all other speakers: his baritone voice! At the end of the day, nature won over technology. I was thoroughly vindicated. Now I could relish again the raucous flippancy in Anthony Thwaite's "The Interpreter," a poem I heard directly from the poet himself in the same year and city where I served as an "official" interpreter thirteen years earlier.

No sooner had the events of the day come to a screeching halt than I uneremoniously hightailed it out of the auditorium and drove home—again with the good Samaritan from Jordan—to sleep and, à la Hamlet, perchance, to dream. "Ay, there's the rub." Indeed, I got something better than I had bargained for: eight hours of log-like, uninterrupted slumber—a rare miracle for me in so many years.

A few days later, I went into my office and found an official envelope on my desk. It was addressed to me with all the punctilious formalities of Arabia. The envelope carried no name of sender. It must be a letter of appreciation, I thought to myself. And perhaps it contained an equitable financial reward for my pains? My heart danced with anticipation—to the accompaniment of Volpone's litany, "Good morning to the day; and next, my gold! / Open the shrine, that I may see my saint." With anxious fingers I opened the neat, thrice-folded letter. To my utterly shocked disillusionment, the envelope carried nothing for me but a rebuke from my department's sergeant-at-arms who, not having been personally informed of my sudden assignment until after the fact, was thus demanding, *ex officio,* a prompt explanation for my "unexcused" absence from my proctoring duty on the morning I was whisked away by higher authorities to moonlight as an interpreter!

Inauguration

BEFORE THE HARVESTING SEASON, Abu Amsha decided to take advantage of the departure of his neighbor Abu Okba to the city and open a straight road in his land. The other route was circuitous and a bit long, so why not save himself the distance of 350 meters at the expense of his enemy and that of the people, the ex-feudal lord Abu Okba? Instead of walking this unnecessary distance, he can use the time to smoke a cigarette and muster his energy, an energy he will use to work his field with spirit and enthusiasm—as reading primers in elementary school say.

Soon after daybreak, Abu Amsha mounted his tractor and opened the road he had wanted in Abu Okba's land—four meters wide, 200 meters long. Then he gathered the sheaves of plowed wheat to make of them a delicious feast for his sheep. When farmers went to their fields, they discovered yet another Agrarian Reform project, single-handedly carried out by an energetic member of their toiling proletarian class behind the back of Abu Okba. Some were saddened to see the sheaves of prematurely harvested wheat scattered on both sides of the new road, while others expressed spiteful delight in what had happened to the former feudal lord Abu Okba.

A small group of brown-nosers consulted among themselves and said, "Abu Okba must be informed about this!" The following morning, each one of them brought whatever he could of the bounties of his land: one brought a sack of tender Armenian cucumbers, another a basket of string beans. A third filled a burlap sack with eggplants—he calls them something too vulgar to be penned down here on paper. His eggplants were of varying sizes: some were small and good for *makdous,* others were medium and good for mahshi, while the rest were edible only for beasts—assuming that beasts really know what's good for them or can appreciate the nutritional value of eggplants. The fourth brown-noser brought two baskets: one had green okras, the other freshly cut mallow leaves. This brown-noser did not know that since the beginning of the Agrarian Reform the enemy of the people was suffering from severe bouts of irritable bowel syndrome, and that for this reason he could not eat any fiber-rich veggies like okra or mallow leaves.

The brown-nosers waited on the public road separating the village houses from the farm lands to take whatever means of transportation to the city. A small van came but had room only for two passengers. The men with Armenian cucumbers and eggplants hopped in, and the other two waited their turn resignedly. The first two heralds arrived at the house of Abu Okba and told him what had happened. He was immediately gripped by abdominal spasms, and so he gulped two Duspatalin* retard tablets, without of course forgetting the dues of hospitality. He offered his guests delicious pieces of *mushabbak* and *shu'aibiyyat*, and so they thanked God for their wise deed, nor did they forget to pray privately for Abu Amsha because he was the reason why they were now eating these city pastries. In the meantime, the other two brown-nosers arrived, having just missed this morning feast. The enemy of the people ordered his persecuted maid to serve black Turkish coffee to all of his guests. The maid offered them the bitter drink, and when the mallows guy took the first sip on an empty stomach—and this was the first time he tasted Turkish coffee—he was rudely surprised by its obnoxious taste, and he involuntarily spat it out on the beautiful white marble floor, saying, "For God's sake, what's this shit?"

In the meantime, Abu Amsha was waiting for a police force to come and arrest him. But he took some precautions. Having opened his desired road, he went in the afternoon to the village blacksmith, and asked him to make him a rectangular iron sheet with two long poles. Then he went to the village pharmacist who was an "alien resident" obliged to serve two years in the countryside after graduation from college. The pharmacist was known for his beautiful penmanship—literally, not figuratively, because the latter would mean that he was an undercover informant—and Abu Amsha told him in whispers that he wanted him to write a few words, "a service to the country," on the metal sheet. The pharmacist promptly answered the call of patriotic duty.

On the third morning, Abu Amsha stood on the public road, waiting for the police to arrive with Abu Okba. He had already instructed his two boys to dig two holes at the beginning of the farm road he had opened two days earlier and to wait for his signal to set up the signpost. He had already prepared some sand, small stones, and half a bag of cement powder for the inauguration of the project. He also readied a ribbon he had torn from his wife's long, worn-out underpants, sent into retirement since the end of the forty days of dead winter—naturally, peasant women know nothing about indecent lingerie like city women—and a pair of iron scissors, too dull to cut even a baby cucumber.

When Abu Amsha spotted the police convoy from afar—he was sharp-eyed even though he was over fifty—he gave his boys the start signal. They quickly mixed the cement with sand and stones, stuck the poles into the two holes, and poured the concrete around them. Abu Okba arrived in his car, accompanied by some brown-nosers, and stopped where Abu Amsha was impatiently waiting for him. The District Chief, a police colonel, and a few of his underlings got off their cars, and the colonel began heaping obscenities—too improper to be documented in this transcript—at Abu Amsha, screaming at him, "What right have you got to transgress against your neighbor and open a road in his land without official permission?" To which Abu Amsha simply said, "Sir, this corrupt feudal lord is not only objecting to the sheer fact of opening the road, but also because I named it after the late Martyr, the Parachutist Staff Major Basil Hafez Al-Assad!"

Abu Okba was speechless, and so was the District Chief. Abu Amsha looked at both of them like someone who wasn't really waiting for an answer. After a delicious moment of suspense, he pointed to the sign board between whose poles the underpants ribbon was flapping, and said to the colonel, "Sir, won't you do me the honor of cutting the ribbon to inaugurate the project? What are you waiting for, Comrade?"

Season of Migration to Switzerland

I DON'T KNOW HOW MY STEPS LED ME TO SWITZERLAND. All I remember is that I got out of one of the Swiss airports (I don't know which one exactly) and headed east. I was walking behind two fellow Arabs, as if pulled by an instinctive magnet. I didn't speak to them, nor did they speak to me. I didn't know their names or which country they were from. Walking behind them, I was inspecting the green Swiss landscape unfolding before my eyes. The greenness didn't strike me as fabulously rich as it had been pictured in our arid desert imagination. Several sheep and a few beautiful goats passed by us, and I was struck by how clean and visibly healthy they were.

While walking behind my fellow Arabs, I noticed a strange kind of onion scattered on my left. Curious, I picked up one and began peeling it. It turned out be some strange kind of garlic I have never seen before: neither like the homegrown garlic we used to have nor like the Chinese garlic we started to import. I peeled one head and tasted it, but it didn't have the taste of garlic I have always known. In fact, it was entirely tasteless. Suddenly, there loomed before me a miserable-looking, blunted hydrant from which a weak trickle was sucked by some sheep hoping to quench their thirst, which I didn't believe anyway. My two fellow Arabs approached and drove the sheep away from the hydrant and began performing their ablution. From this silent act, I gathered that it was time for prayer (but which one exactly I did not know). When the second one finished his ablution, I moved forward to perform mine. When I began to distribute the weak trickle of water on my left foot, suddenly appeared a dark skinned fellow Arab, attired in Gulf clothing and with an untrimmed beard. He began to wash off the mud stuck in his cracked foot and shoes on my left foot. He neither spoke to me, nor did I to him. I didn't even object to what he was doing. Perhaps I just wanted to catch up with my two fellows who have already walked a respectable distance during my ablution. I don't know how I managed to get rid of the blessings of his grace.

I saw many minarets in every direction, and wondered how that came to be after the Swiss government's decision to remove them. At any rate, I privately decided that I would pray with my two fellows in the nearest mosque on the right, whether they liked it or not. I got tired of following them, and I did not wish to walk to a remote mosque just because it might be bigger or finer. I also felt that my bladder was fidgeting under its unbearable store.

Despite the evidently numerous minarets, my two companions insisted on knocking at the door of a house to ask about a mosque. They didn't tell me their intention, but I understood it as if by telepathy. I wanted to show them the numerous mosques nearby, but my voice was beyond my tongue's reach. They knocked at the door of a one-story house with a red-tiled roof at the foot of a small hill, a few steps below ground level. Two small blonde girls, around seven years old and looking like twins, came out and began chattering with my fellows. I didn't hear what the girls were saying but I gathered that they were originally from my own country. While the four were talking, the owner of the house came out of the garage, with aggressiveness writ large on his face. He didn't take the cement steps leading up to the foothill, but jumped from the tiled floor of his front yard to the grassy knoll, and headed towards me. I was the farthest of the three from his house and girls. He barked at me, "I know these types that come to this country. You're all thieves and highwaymen." He was in his mid-forties and had a neatly trimmed beard, half of which was already gray, while the other half was struggling for black survival. His clothes indicated that he was playing golf before he found me in the precincts of his house.

With a lightning move, he put his hand in the right pocket of my pants, and snatched out the wrist watch my wife had given me five or six years ago on our wedding anniversary. I was surprised how he found it in my pocket when I wore it only for a few days to please my wife, and then I said to her that I hated to burden my wrist with a superfluous accessory that lost its practical value after the advent of cellphones. He put it on his left hand and began looking at it admiringly. Good lord in heaven, this man lives in the capital of world watchmaking, likes none other than the watch he usurps from me, yet he accuses me of being a thief and a highwayman! I wanted to ask him to return my watch to me, but he shook it in my face provocatively as if to say, "In your dreams!" Suddenly, the tie on my tongue was loosened, and I was taken aback by the torrent of words that started flying like a news bulletin on a state-owned satellite channel, now temporarily headquartered in my head.

Under the pressure of my about-to-explode bladder, I said to him, "Listen, you extremist fundamentalist and hired infiltrator, I too know the likes of you. Give me back my watch or I'll give you a slap you'll never forget as long as you live."

"And what if I don't?" he asked me defiantly.

Here my right hand shot reflexively to his willy and squeezed it to make him understand that I mean what I say. Words followed swiftly in the heels of my deed, "I'll press charges of theft against you, and you might lose your beautiful stay here in this neutral country. And if you lose your earthly heaven and go back home, you know where you'll end up."

"And where will you end up?" he asked derisively.

"Personally, I'm going back home, anyway, and I have nothing to worry about . . . except . . . except . . . my bladder."

I didn't have the chance to see the surprise on my interlocutor's face or even to comprehend my own last words because I really woke up then under pressure from my bladder, only to find that I was holding my hurting willy too tightly—lest I flood myself. I ran to the bathroom and emptied my bladder quickly so as to get back to bed and resume the untimely interrupted first round of national dialogue between me and my compatriot.

Love Meter

ON THE FIRST DAY OF THE SECOND SEMESTER, his fifth-grade son came home from school and served him with a fiat, "Dad, you must buy me a laptop."

"Who says I must?"

"The computer class teacher."

"Why?"

"So that I can apply at home what I learn at school."

"Well, son, you know things are a bit tight these days, but you are welcome to use our home computer."

"I said I wanted a laptop, not a desktop. Plus, mom spends so much time on it during the day, and in the evening it is your turn."

"True, but I have to work to put bread on the table for you, your two sisters, mom—and a few more people less fortunate than we."

"Who is less fortunate than we?"

"Your aunts and uncles in Syria, for instance."

"By the way, Dad, when can we go back to Syria and live again in our own home?"

"When the war is over, and your eldest uncle can stand on his feet again."

At this point, Samar, who has been reading the news online, butted in. She started brawling and storming, "He's your only son and you find it too much to buy him a laptop?" She didn't say our only son, but your only son! He knew at once that he would be fighting a losing battle. So he immediately entered into negotiations with her and the little brat—just to wait until he received next month's salary. To which they triumphantly agreed. His next salary was just around the corner, anyway.

At the beginning of the month he had to factor his son's laptop into the budget. In addition to the regular payments, expenses, rent, and the occasional transfers to his now unemployed brother in Syria, he also had a bank loan to pay back—a backbreaking one which automatically deducts a big chunk of his salary as soon as it is deposited by his construction company. Before the start of the war, he had just spent all his savings to furnish their family residence back home. And during his last visit there, when their hometown was still relatively peaceful, a mortar shell from the 17th Infantry Division landed on their garage and destroyed his Kuwaiti-licensed car, so they ran for their lives. Back in Kuwait, he had to take a loan in order to buy a new car to replace the old one he had lost.

And now the cheapest kid laptop was about four hundred dollars. He can't possibly make ends meet. He tried to back out of the deal, but he ran into a wall. The war back home had also made everyone so edgy. His wife's ultimatum settled the back-and-forth, "If we can't live in a place of our own, if I can't buy jewelry, the least you can buy us is a laptop."

He wondered if the hussy has ever read Hemingway's story "Cat in the Rain" in Arabic translation. Okay, Memsahib, your brat shall have his laptop, but no Mannlicher for you, for I plan to be no Francis Macomber.

Well, to cut a story short, he finally bought a laptop for his son—to get the Memsahib off his back. Several evenings later, the brat told them about an online application called "Love Meter" he had heard about from his classmates. It is supposed to calculate the percentage of love between two people, and that all you have to do is enter their names. So his son entered his name and that of his youngest sister Najla, and the percentage given was 96%. An amazing percentage, and very probable too. Then he entered his name and that of his other sister, Amal, with whom he really had a sibling rivalry, and the computer gave an alarming 27%. Amal started to cry and her father had a hell of a time calming her down, telling her that the computer was a liar, etc.

While he was busy comforting his daughter, his brat of a son started to giggle. Then he beckoned to his mother to come and see something on his screen. The wife was surprised and she asked her husband with an accusing scowl on her face, "What's this?"

Without moving from his place on the sofa, he asked her, "What's what?"

"Well, come over and see for yourself."

He went and she pointed to a percentage on the screen. It was a shamelessly low percentage, but until then it didn't occur to him to look at the pair of names entered. He did so only when she asked, "How do you explain this?"

"Explain what?"

"Your lack of love for me."

"Do you really believe this nonsense?"

"Of course, I do. You have already seen two accurate results. There is no denying that Rami loves his youngest sister more than the other."

"Honey, come on, you know I love you."

"How much?"

"A lot."

"I mean: what percentage?"

"I can't quantify it."

"That's because you don't love me 100%."

"Well, there are a few things in you I wish were different, but I love you nonetheless. You're my wife and the mother of my children. We've been happily married for twelve years. We didn't need an online application when we fell in love and got married."

But she was sulking, and the pouting became more of a permanent fixture of her face. He was flabbergasted. This damned laptop caused an unnecessary warfare. He felt like slapping his son for this nasty gimmick. Then it dawned on him. If his idea worked, then he'd convince his wife that computers could never accurately gauge human feelings, and he wouldn't need to slap his brat.

He told his son to bring him the laptop, and, entering one name then another, he hit the Enter key. And, voila, the result was just what he was hoping for. So he erased the names and moved over to his wife, but she refused to look at him. The funny thing is that when he looked at her face, it looked to him more like a computer screen than a lovely wife's face. After several more attempts, she relented. He entered the word "cat" in the top box and "dog" in the bottom one. Before he hit the Enter key, he asked her, "Is there any possibility that these two can ever love each other?" She said, "No."

At this point, he hit Enter and beamed with expectant triumph. The percentage was ninety-three or something like that. Dead silence. His wife had a poker face by now. He waved his hand in front of her face, but she didn't even bat.

"So?" he asked encouragingly.

"You see, even the love percentage between dogs and cats is higher than your love for me!"

He wanted to pull his hair in despair but then remembered that he was completely bald. To make up for the missed joy of pulling his hair, he wondered, Why am I supposed to be the guilty one here? What if she is the one who is failing in the dues of love? But he didn't want to aggravate things. He also knew she would speechify about her own stoic sacrifice, "Remember, I dropped out of college because I was madly in love and I couldn't wait to marry you." That has always been his silencer.

They agreed to try names of historically famous couples in love. They began with Qays and Laila, and the love meter gave a high reading. The same was with Antar and Abla. She suggested Romeo and Juliet, but he objected on grounds that these might simply be fictional characters, and therefore, whatever reading the computer gave, it would be questionable. But she insisted, and he had to comply. Again the percentage given was in favor of his wife's pontifications. She quipped, "You see?"

He asked her, "Who's the computer engineer here?"

"Who else? Why do you ask?"

"Honey, I know that any computer program regurgitates only what's programmed in it. Perhaps the programmers who created this diabolic monster fed into it names of famous people, both fictional and real, who were in love, which explains why you always get the same percentage whenever you enter the same pair of names. What if there is a contemporary couple also named Qays and Laila, but, unlike the historical couple we know from classical lore, they hated each other? How does the computer program know which couple I have in mind when I ask it to measure their love?"

She maintained that unnerving look of pouting hurt.

He asked her, "Which one was the Prophet Muhammad's favorite wife?"

"Aysha."

"Exactly. Now let's try their names and see if the computer can give us an approximate idea of how much the prophet loved Aysha."

"Okay."

So he entered the names and the result was a scandalous 32%.

"Now, do you still trust this love meter?"

"I don't know anymore. Maybe what we need to reconsider is those reports about the prophet's. . . "

"For God's sake, don't turn a revisionist historian on me now just to score a point."

He was drained, his home away from home—the latter now being war-torn—was also ripped apart by some cyber devil. He wanted to slap his son and, for good measure, his computer class teacher as well. But there was simply no point in making more enemies. I should have sent that brat to a public school where this computer nonsense is postponed until much later when, it is hoped, my wife wouldn't be so shell-shocked as to feel persecuted.

His wife withdrew to a corner of the living room and sulked there, satisfied in the knowledge of being vindicated in her victimhood. The week dragged on, without any one of them showing a desire for patching up. They were in that classical marital stalemate where both partners feel, I haven't done anything wrong, so why should I be the one to apologize? A wall of ice rose between them. Since the fight, his wife has slept on a mattress in the girls' room. If they passed each other in the hallway, or sat down for dinner, they maintained their self-satisfied mopey appearance.

On Thursday evening, after dinner, his youngest daughter snuggled up to him and said, "Dad, will you please roast me those chestnuts you bought last weekend?" Tears welled up in his eyes. He remembered how his late mother used to do that for them when they were little kids, and how, when she died two years ago, he couldn't travel to attend her funeral. The country was too bedeviled by war, and his brothers and sisters didn't want him to risk his life by crossing the border.

He heated the oven, cracked the chestnut shells with a sharp knife, and placed them in a pan, which he shoved into the oven, and waited for a few minutes. His daughter was excited by the little explosions inside the oven. He pulled the pan out and put it on the table. He called the kids and told Rami to call his mom, and after some reluctance she accepted the invitation. He sat at the head of the table, and his wife took her usual place on his left, and next to her sat Amal. On his right was Najla. Rami, the trouble maker, sat across the table from his father. Amal and Najla needed help cracking the hot chestnuts. So it fell to the parents to serve the girl next to them. His wife was more adroit at shelling than he was, so when she noticed that Najla wasn't getting enough, every now and then she would reach out and offer her one of the hot goodies. "A one-upmanship to make up for my incompetence," he thought.

He plodded on with his cracking business as best as he could. He shelled a nicely roasted plump heart. He was planning to hand it to Najla, but Amal asked to have it instead. He looked at Najla inquiringly and she said, "It's OK, Dad. She can have it." At this very moment, his wife was deftly shelling another nicely roasted plump heart and had all the intention to give it to Najla. She reached out to Najla at the same time he reached out to Amal, and their hands collided in mid-air above the table. Both hearts fell, and each girl grabbed the one that fell closest to her. They actually didn't notice that as a result of this mid-air collision, the exchange of hearts was unintentionally aborted. One more thing: he briefly skimmed his wife's warm fingers, and a vague nostalgia was rekindled. The ice in his heart also began to thaw. He has been avoiding looking at her straight since the beginning of their cyber war. And whenever he stole a furtive glance at her face during their weeklong sulking embitterment, he saw the same computer screen still there. Now, slowly they began to look at each other less furtively.

Rami had the last chestnut in hand. He cracked it open, then took a knife, and quartered it into four nearly equal pieces. He offered two pieces to his younger sisters, and two to his mom and dad. His father was touched and felt the iceberg melting fast. He looked at his wife and saw that she was not vindictive but proud. Then the rascal assumed his occasional second-father tone and comically commanded, "Come on, kids. Time for bed." He winked at his father and said, "Good luck with your boss." He wanted to hit him with something soft but none was within reach, and the rascal vroomed to his bedroom and closed the door. His sisters followed suit to theirs.

Alone with his wife, he hugged her tightly. Traipsing softly to the bedroom, he told her teasingly, "Wait. Let's try that love meter program again. Maybe, it will give us a better reading this time!" She grabbed his good old "harrow"—which in the early days of their marriage she alternatively called "the one and only joystick"—and said, "Here in my hand I have a concrete love meter."

Lost Snails

After the breezes of the Arab Spring rose, and two Arab pharaohs fell with the speed of light—measured, of course, by the Arab chronometer—Abu Jihad and his family decided to return home and put an end to several years of living abroad. Perhaps, they too could reap the ripe fruits of their prospective summer and celebrate their dream apartment which they have been getting ready and furnishing all those years abroad.

About a month after their return, they were sitting in front of the TV and watching the developments of Arab revolts, switching from one satellite channel whose coverage of events doesn't please them to another one that tickles their feelings, touches their dreams, and makes the much awaited victory just around the next newsflash. Suddenly, Abu Jihad saw his youngest daughter Maha standing in the middle of the handmade rug his mother has woven especially to commemorate his return. The baby came from the big living room in which she has been playing. Groaning and writhing in pain, the poor thing was pointing to her belly with her little fingers. Their eyes were too focused on the screen in front of them to take notice of her; plus the semi words she was attempting were too babyishly cute to be taken seriously.

All of a sudden, they were inundated with a rotten, obnoxious smell. The horrid stench drew their eyes to two steady trickles from the baby's diaper, running down the inside of her beautiful round thighs, and forming a greenish pool around her feet in the middle of the rug. During their years abroad, they have forgotten that the Euphrates was no longer what it was, that its water was no longer drinkable, thanks to the sewage the city dumps into it. Unused to its stagnant, contaminated water, the poor little creature had a severe enterosepsis. She felt guilty when she saw red eyes staring at her and heard sharp tongues condemning what she did. When her mother rushed towards her, cursing the hour they decided to return, the disheartened girl raised her right hand above her little head and exclaimed audibly, "Allah, Iya, Tatu, bass!" They unmistakably understood the first and last words, and guessed the other two from the slogans unfailingly reiterated in the "spontaneous" pro-Assad demonstrations staged by the intelligence every blessed Friday.

Abu Jihad took the rug to the nearest laundromat. The clerk asked him about the nature of the dirty spot, and he told him that it could be simply cleaned with a little hot water and good detergents. The clerk charged a certain amount, and Abu Jihad offered him double that provided he rid him of that damned spot. A few days later, Abu Jihad went to the laundromat to collect his mother's rug. At home, he unrolled the rug—only to find the horrid smell simply overpowered by the scent of detergents. He still had doubts that it was stuck immovably there, what with the still visible traces of the spot in the middle of the rug. He said to his wife, "Nothing scratches the skin like one's own fingernail." To which she responded, "Oh really? You expect me, after all those years of living abroad, to clean your mother's rug with my own hands?" The spot remained rooted in the middle of the white rug like a black raven's shit on white marble.

The natural cycle of spring was over, and summer started, but the media extended the bailiwick of the Arab Spring another season, regardless of the climate changes. Language was divorced from its familiar signification, and numerous masks fell. Secularists turned sectarian, and comedy stars, who in the past warmed the hearts of their audience with their avant-gardist art, turned out to be no better than barking clowns in the service of criminality, repression, and corruption; while modernists and fundamentalists were two faces of the same coin.

Abu Jihad deserted his conjugal bed and started to sleep in front of the TV, afraid that he might, in a moment of oblivion, miss an important Breaking News in this spring of nothing but pools of blood and piles of skulls. And then he would hear the taunts of his wife when calling the kids, "Bring me the remote. I want to see what my co-wife is showing to your father today." Abu Jihad would then take refuge in helpless, impotent silence. At midnight, another battle breaks out over the remote, this time between him and his daughter Afaf. He wants to watch episodes of the Arab Spring; she wants to see the Mexican telenovela Cuidado con el Ángel, known to Arab audiences as Marichuy.

One day he imposed his will on everyone and forced them to watch an episode of the Arab Spring telenovela. And why not? Doesn't it have enough murder, destruction, wars, charging camels, mules, police dogs, donkeys, blood, torn-out bellies, amputated limbs, slit throats, children's fingernails brutally extracted, howling, and screaming—all carried live and for free without any attempt at polishing their crudity? Not impressed by Arab action films, Afaf yawned and whined, "Oh, poor me. By God, I should be crying day and night for the way you treat me!" The silent majority kept silent, but he felt their secret gloating because in a few months he fell, in the eyes of Afaf, from being Papa the Honey to Papa Somoza.

A few days later, Abu Jihad was coming back home and carrying a few things for breakfast. He found little Maha lying on his mattress in front of the TV, and she beamed delightfully when she saw him. Her brother Jihad, seven years her senior, lay down next to her and began to tease and jostle her. She screamed in protest and wanted him out of the bed. Forced out by his father, he recited, "They say: Surely, if we return to Al-Madinah the mightier will soon drive out the weaker; but the hypocrites know not."

His angry father replied, "You misquoted God who says, 'They say: Surely, if we return to Al-Madinah the mightier will soon drive out the weaker; when might belongeth to Allah and to His messenger and to the believers; but the hypocrites know not.'"

"That's what I learned at school!" Jihad said.

"You don't know the holy Quran well enough, yet you don't hesitate to use it to threaten your little sister, you rascal?"

The father didn't find it funny to hear his son say that to his younger sister, even though he was confident of his deep love for her. On the contrary, he saw in his misquote a seed of a terrifying, evil plant.

Afaf came yawning and said, "Dad, are girls circumcised like boys?"

"Who told you that?"

"Yesterday, I saw people on TV shouting, 'The people—want—to circumcise—girls,' and I was scared. I hope they are not going to circumcise me like Jihad?"

"No, sweetheart, the people were saying, 'The people want to purify the country' not girls. That is, the people want to clean the country of its filth."

Abu Jihad saw the terror in the eyes of his young girl who thought that the people wanted to circumcise girls. He said to himself, "What a miserable revolution that has no other goal than the circumcision of girls! I wonder if anyone else misunderstood the slogan chanted by demonstrators on that sad, bloody Friday?"

"Get our suitcases ready to pack up," he boomed at his wife.

"Where to?"

"Back to our self-imposed exile!"

"What happened to you, man? Are you crazy? Haven't we had enough of wandering here and there like roaming nomads?"

In fact, he was never more clear-headed than he was now. He had just realized that exile was his only homeland, that the little he possessed in his native country did not justify calling it home, that he did not have enough hope to sustain him through the balance of his dark days on this earth, that the opposition factions—comfortably lounged in luxurious hotels abroad, while inciting civilians to defy repressive regimes and their criminal organs with open chests—did not seek freedom for the oppressed, but were power-hungry fortune-hunters, peddling dreams and illusions to the poor masses. And here they are today fighting over trifles, each hoping to build a country for itself with the skulls and bones of the simple, the naïve, and the duped.

He stared at his wife, then whispered to the distant horizon, "We're lost snails carrying our homes on our backs."

Then he turned to his wife and said, "Come on, let's pack!"

"I'm packing nothing. If you wish, you can divorce me."

"We're staying with Mom."

"Okay, then. And I will have my mother's rug, the rug you soiled."

He carried the rug to the kids' room. Then he placed a chair under the ceiling fan, swung a rope around its blades, and at its dangling end he made a noose big enough to be slipped around the neck of a snail which all of a sudden perceived what it has never perceived before. He sent his brother a text message saying, "When these my words reach you, wrap me up in mother's rug, bury my naked corpse under wing of darkness in the middle of the river, and weight me down with a rock." His brother will at first think that he is trying his hand at a modernist poem. No harm in that thought—temporarily. Out of precaution, he put his cellphone on silent lest it alert someone before he could carry out his plan. He mounted the chair, slipped the noose around his neck, kicked the chair with his feet, and hanged himself.

In Memory of Yousef

THE PUBLICATION OF *THE CRY OF A PEN* by poet Jihad Samawi created a big furor among anti-regime literati and media pundits. As I gathered from the media reports, the volume contained fiery poems that attacked repression, despotism, and corruption in Syria. What boosted the popularity of Samawi's book was that he was also the founder of Fairness Forum, one of civil society's many bodies that had once mushroomed in the country when dreamers were under the illusion that the heir apparent would not follow the example of his autocratic father. But, like many disillusioned others, Samawi fled into exile which afforded him a freedom of expression he could not dream of had he stayed confined within his country.

A few years ago, I had met Samawi at his maternal uncle's house in our self-imposed exile. His uncle Yousef was an old friend and former colleague of mine. But despite the furor created by Samawi's *The Cry of a Pen*, I didn't get to read it.

During my last trip to Istanbul, I was once having lunch at an Arabic restaurant. When I went to pay the bill, someone grabbed my shoulders from behind with such heavy hands as if he were in a wrestling match trying to bring his opponent into a submission hold. I am no wrestler, so what does this bully want from a weak man like me? I turned around in panic only to find myself face to face with the media celeb Jihad Samawi. Before I greeted him, it occurred to me: How could a poet have such big hands? I haven't noticed their size when I first met him at his uncle's.

He said with evident surprise and joy, "So, you are one of our restaurant's clientele! A thousand welcomes to you!"

In reply, I asked him naively, "Your restaurant?"

I had forgotten that before his uncle died he had told me this nephew of his opened a fancy restaurant in Istanbul. In fact, what lured me to this restaurant, which I found by accident, was neither its elegant décor nor the menu displayed at its entrance in Arabic, Turkish, and English. No, it was its curious name: "Tip of the Pen." What a name for a restaurant!

Samawi prevented me from paying the one-hundred lira bill, saying, "For shame, man, this is an insult to me. You are my guest at Tip of the Pen as long as you are in Istanbul."

He force-led me to the VIP lounge in the restaurant and ordered a cup of coffee—extra sugar—for me.

He said, "My uncle, Gold bless his soul, used to tell me a lot about you since you were both in college."

"He too told me about you," said I, "but shortly before he died. God bless his soul."

A dark cloud suddenly formed itself over Samawi's bright forehead, and he began rubbing his neck nervously.

When the coffee he had ordered for me came, I pushed the cup towards him. He asked me, "Don't you drink coffee? This cup is for you!"

"You ordered the coffee the way you, not I, like it," said I. "That's why I think you are more entitled to it than I am."

He was slightly embarrassed by this diplomatic faux pas on his part and also because of my incisive candor. This time he ordered the coffee the way I like it. Just black coffee.

He said with a contrived guffaw, "I like your candor—perhaps that was why my uncle had befriended you. And speaking of candor, I want to tell you about an idea that has been occupying my mind for quite some time, but my uncle's sudden death has severed the only link of communication with you, thus leaving my idea unrealized."

"Go ahead," I said. "I'm all ears."

"What do you think of my collection of poetry, *The Cry of a Pen,* published three years ago?"

"I didn't read it, though I read bits and pieces about it."

"Oh, how come?" he whined, feigning hurt.

"Blame it on circumstances."

"That's alright. I have a proposal for you: How about translating the collection into English?"

I showed no response.

"Do you have the will to do that?"

"That depends on our reaching a satisfactory agreement to all parties concerned."

"Excellent. How much do you normally charge per page?"

"I charge thirty dollars per page regardless of how many lines are in it."

He made quick calculations in his head, then said, "And won't you give the nephew of your dearest friend a break?"

"Of course! Why not? How many pages are there in *The Cry of a Pen?*"

"One hundred fifty-five pages."

In this five-word reply, he made two silly grammatical mistakes, which I candidly pointed out to him. At first, he tried to stand on his wounded dignity and also to capitalize on his fame as a media personality to discredit my corrections. But I ignored all of that humbug and went on to explain to him the simple points of grammar that are usually taught in elementary school. He was rendered speechless for an awkward moment.

"Now I realize, more than ever before, why my uncle admired you."

"Bless his soul. He has been finally relieved of life and its people."

"You still didn't tell me how much you would charge me per page."

"In honor of the memory of Yousef, I am going to charge you only for 150 pages instead of 155."

He made quick calculations in his head again and said, "So you are going to charge me 4,500 dollars?"

"No, that would be the fare I normally charge to a client I don't know really well. Now, because I know you, I can't help honoring the memory of my friend and your uncle."

"God bless you. I can't thank you enough."

"I don't think you will need to."

Mystified, he looked up at me quizzically.

"Poet Laureate Samawi," I said in sugar-coated sarcasm, "I won't charge you more than 150,000 dollars!"

"Well, my uncle never mentioned you are also a joker."

"That's right. I'm not joking with you. By God, I am not."

He was tongue-tied by shock for a moment before he became chatty again.

"How could a translator charge 150,000 dollars for the translation of a worthless collection of poetry?"

He made the same silly grammatical mistakes again but corrected himself in mid-sentence.

"I didn't say this was the fare I would charge you for my own sweat."

"I don't understand you. You are speaking in riddles. Please talk to me plainly, candidly!"

"Honestly, I'm willing to translate *The Cry of a Pen,* your worthless collection by your own admission, at no charge at all, but I will accept nothing short of the 150,000 dollars."

"My God, you're still speaking in riddles!"

"Listen, I don't want the 150,000 dollars for me. No, I want to take this money from you and give it back to your uncle's orphaned children—the very uncle from whom you had borrowed this sum to open your fancy Tip of the Pen, the very uncle you heartlessly ignored when he had repeatedly begged you to pay him back just enough to undergo a simple surgery to unblock his urethra, the very uncle who suffered for several months until his kidneys failed, the very uncle whose long distance calls to you were so unbearable that you changed your number, the very uncle who, seeing you on TV screens passionately defending the rights of the oppressed, *les misérables,* died of a stroke, of too much oppression at your own hands, Monseigneur Hugo! Or should I call you Fanon because Hugo is too white for your subaltern taste?"

"Apparently, I mistook you for someone else."

"Apparently? No, Sir, certainly."

I stood up and left him, mouth agape. At the entrance to Tip of the Pen, I found a scrawny little girl—the age of Yousef's daughter—begging. I fished out of my pocket the one-hundred lira banknote I had intended to pay for the lunch I had at Samawi's royal hideout. Handing it to the overjoyed poor thing, I whispered, "In memory of Yousef."

Dew and Rain

"WHAT ARE YOUR FUTURE PLANS?" was the last question I had to answer for an interview with the editor of a local publication. Future plans? I don't know what tomorrow, let alone the future, holds for me! The question sounded somewhat frivolous. For the past few years, my life, though stable by all appearances, has been one worry-laden career. Not least of my worries was the possibility of getting my residence in Saudi Arabia abruptly terminated or having my Syrian passport not renewed. I wanted to say, "To be able someday to go back to Syria and die there." Since my last visit to the country five years ago, dying in exile loomed as a worse prospective than spending a life in exile. Not wishing to sound facetiously melodramatic, however, I resisted the silly temptation and wrote instead, "To finish translating Zora Neale Hurston's novel Their Eyes Were Watching God." I am watching God, too—and hoping against hope for a bright tomorrow. In the meantime, translation would be a cathartic diversion.

The following day, at around 4:00 pm, I came home after a brief outing with my wife. All of our four kids were blissfully napping. I, too, could use a good nap. As I headed to the bedroom, my cellphone rang. I looked at the calling number, and I felt the knot in my lower abdomen tightening worse than before. For the past few days, I have been suffering from relentless abdominal spasms. And this morning they got worse and worse. I put the spasms down to stress and too much coffee. There was also the impending attack by US-backed Syrian Democratic Forces (SDF) on ISIS-held territories, where my extended family lived. My anxiety was further aggravated by lack of communication with them. And I had to rely on the quicksands of social media and hearsay. Our countryside has been relatively safe so far, and in the past I have often congratulated myself for having built a beautiful country house in our native village, to which my eldest brother and his family have fled to escape aerial bombardment on Raqqa, the usurped capital of ISIS. Alerted by a local rat that "the apostate's villa" had been "illegally requisitioned by a squatter," ISIS had summarily kicked my brother and his family out, confiscated the house, and turned it into a detention center. My brother's last WhatsApp message to me said, "Now we envy the dead, for they are spared what we have seen and heard!"

Abu Khalil, calling from Dubai, asked in a broken voice, "Have you heard any news from back home?" I only had a flat no for a reply. Then he said he had received news that my friend and distant relative Dr Sami was killed in an American air raid on his house. Dr Sami, originally a native of Aleppo, was the only doctor who remained behind in the village, while his wife and children, except his eldest son who escaped to France, fled to Damascus.

"But why the raid on his house?" I asked.

"Oh, he was just collateral damage," explained Abu Khalil.

I quizzed him further, and he told me that about a hundred meters from the doctor's house, there was an ISIS hisba center.

Just as I hung up with Abu Khalil, I received a WhatsApp message from the only nephew of mine still serving in Assad's army—a conscript who once tried to defect but was arrested, then jailed and brutally tortured for six months. He, too, reported the sad news of Dr Sami's death. The doctor's house was only a few hundred meters away from mine. By local standards, my house looked luxurious enough to attract any invader, while its occupation by ISIS made it a prime target for aerial bombardment. I was worried for my brothers and sisters and their droves of children, and wondered if they managed to flee and where to. I asked Abu Khalil but he had no idea. Unless held as human shields, they couldn't possibly stay in the crossfire. And if they had entertained any illusion about the good will of the new invaders/ liberators and their backers, the raid on Dr Sami's house must have been enough of an eye opener.

For the next eight hours I was on the phone with relatives in Syria, Lebanon, and Turkey, trying to get solid information. While thus occupied, I received a phone call from Germany. I read 'Regen calling' on my cellphone screen. Regen? I don't know anyone in Germany named Regen. And how did he end up in my contacts? When I answered, the caller said in Arabic, "Hello, Uncle. This is Matar or Regen." Oh, it was that Matar, whose mother is my cousin. I have forgotten that since his escape to Germany two years ago, I had jokingly nicknamed him Regen, which is only the German equivalent of the Arabic name Matar (Rain). He, too, was desperate for information about his wife, many kids, and widowed mother (recently gone blind because ISIS would not allow her to leave for Damascus to seek treatment). I had nothing to allay his fears. I sent a desperate WhatsApp message to Dr Sami's number, hoping that someone would answer me. Citizens, trapped in areas beyond the bailiwick of "useful Syria," could only send and receive messages via WhatsApp and other free-calling applications.

Reports about Dr Sami's fate kept coming and were maddeningly contra-dictory. One report says he is confirmed dead, others say he is still alive. One report says he died a natural death by a heart attack, another claims his house was bombarded by mistake but he was only severely wounded and that, since all bridges on the Euphrates were recently destroyed by the Inter-national Coalition warplanes, he was ferried on a crude raft across the river for treatment, south of the river. There was equally no solid news about the whereabouts of my extended family. One report says they fled to the northern bank of the Euphrates (at least they won't die of thirst there); another says they escaped to the wilderness north of the village.

At 8:00 am the following morning, I received a message on my Facebook Messenger from someone named Nada Al-Sabah (ie Morning Dew). It was a familiar pseudonym on my Facebook page, but I never knew to whom it belonged. It turned out to be Nada, Dr Sami's eldest daughter, texting from Damascus and asking me for news about her father. I could no longer remember what she looked like or how old she was now. How can I tell her what I have already heard? Did she read the social media reports about her father's death? Thank goodness, her questions were too general and did not clearly indicate that she has heard anything awful. I feigned total ignorance and assured her that I would call her as soon as I had any news. Of course, I wouldn't be the first one to communicate the tragic news should it become necessary.

For the rest of the morning, I busied myself with proofreading two trans-lations of mine scheduled for publication in Abu Dhabi before the Book Fair there in six weeks from now. Before going to pick up my two daughters from school, I went to a nearby pharmacy and bought another anti-spasmodic medication. At 12:45 pm, I drove to school. During the three-minute drive, I heard two successive messages beeping in my pocket, and I was both scared and anxious to look. As soon as I parked the car near the school, I checked my cellphone and found that it was Nada telling me that her father's reported death was just a rumor, and that he was only slightly scratched here and there. I sighed with relief. I started calling everyone who cared about the doctor and relayed the good news. Soon other messages began pouring in, confirming that the good doctor was alive and kicking.

About half an hour later, I received news of a confirmed tragedy. Two boys, both sixteen years old, were riding a motor bike among the refugees scattered in the wilderness north of the village. They drove over a land mine that had been planted by ISIS to deter any attackers. When the mine went off, one boy was killed on the spot, the other had one of his legs amputated. The amputee was none other than the son of Matar—or Regen/ Rain—who had called me the night before from Germany and was desperately looking for news about his family and relatives.

A few days later I heard that my country house changed occupiers: clearing it of mines left by ISIS, the SDF turned it into "a command center." About six weeks later, Dr Sami answered my WhatsApp message and told me that he was heading to Damascus to join his refugee family, and that his reported death was simply a rumor spread by ill-wishers. He denied that his country house and clinic were ever bombed. The following day marked the beginning of Ramadan. Dr Sami, accompanied by his five-year old son, strolled to a nearby mosque from his grungy apartment in Damascus—rented at an extortionate price—to pray *taraweeh,* an extended prayer observed in congregation during the evenings of Ramadan. Before reaching the mosque, he dropped dead of a heart attack.

Gilgamesh and
the Young White Elephant

Soon after the total surrender of Babylonia to the rule of the
Achaemenid Persians, the military governor of Uruk had a young white
elephant shipped to him from India. The spoiled elephant wreaked havoc with
the crops of the colonized Babylonian farmers, but how can they ever protest
against the pet of their newly installed despot? After discussing the matter, the
elders of Uruk decided to send a delegation of twenty men—led by a young
chap named Gilgamesh—to the Achaemenid governor. With Gilgamesh at
their head, the delegation set off—all determined to say, "Enough is enough!"
They carried red banners with statements denouncing the elephant's trans-
gressions. People told them to turn back, but they just ignored them at first.
They marched on, and other cynics told them, "You'll get nowhere with this."
They did not listen. On they marched for another mile, and hecklers said,
"They've set a trap for you, you fools." But Gilgamesh turned a deaf ear to
the councils of the nervous nellies of Uruk—determined not to be derailed
from his course. When he had arrived at the gate of the massive palace, he
turned around and, lo and behold, only his close friend Enkidu remained of
the delegation! From far off, he could make out the figure of an old woman
waving to him with a white sack.

"What do you want, mother?"
"A little flour, my son."
"Go back, and—Marduk willing—you shall lack nothing from now on."

Gilgamesh and his friend Enkidu requested permission to see the governor
and they were admitted.

"May the Anunnaki bless you," said Gilgamesh.
"What do you want, you peasants?"
"We come to offer you advice, my Lord."
"Advice from peasants whose country we occupy?"
"Well, my Lord, you see—we are kind of leaders among our own folks. If
you wish, we can share with you our humble thoughts."
"Okay, I'm all ears."

"My Lord, you have a beautiful white elephant—may Marduk give him long life—and he is adored by our people who have been lately honored by your administration of their country. We two have been delegated by our own folks to come and beg you to bring a young female elephant so that she could keep our adored idol company and perhaps the two of them, with the will of Ishtar, can grace our land with their noble seed."

"Well said, smart peasant. How shall we reward you?"

"My Lord, I've plenty of winter and summer food supplies. How about appointing me your brave army's food supplier?"

"Provided that you sell them to us at half their market price."

"So it pleases Ashnan."

"Does your friend have anything to offer us also?"

"Yes, in Phoenicia there is a monster, named Humbaba, guarding the cedar forest. May I, my Lord, humbly suggest that you send an army under the command of Enkidu to kill the monster? If Enkidu succeeds in killing Humbaba, you will appoint him Chief Woodcutter in the cedar forest. And if I may also bring to your attention that cedar-wood is the best for ship building. Who knows, perhaps one day you may wish to push your frontiers as far west as Carthage."

"Well, I must admit that it has never occurred to us that we could find, among you peasants, such smart and sensible followers."

The Secret History of a Dog

O UR FATHER DIED WHEN THE ELDEST among us was only fourteen. And apart from God, he left us nothing to support us but a few sheep, on whose milk and yoghurt we lived, and a small piece of land we planted with wheat in winter and vegetables in summer. His sudden departure left a void in us, the young ones, and a lasting ache in mother's heart. A few months later, my maternal uncle Khaddour came and began talking to my mother in whispers, and she shook her head in disapproval. Uncle Khaddour was persistent, and he was incredulously gesticulating and pouting in counter-disapproval. All of a sudden, we saw her picking up a stick in front of her and bringing it down on his head. But he sprang to his feet in time, as if stung, and ran away, saying, "Obstinate heifer!" We understood nothing then of what transpired between uncle and mother, but she began hugging us one by one, and crying so bitterly even little Hassoun cried in sympathy. In the evening, Sammour, my youngest paternal uncle, came and disdainfully told my mother to look for some other man to thresh her granary. Before we retired to bed, Imad and I drew a profile picture of our maternal uncle, giving him the neck of an ostrich and the eyes of a locust.

The following morning, mother sent my brother Imad to my paternal uncle Haleem, begging him to send one of his older sons to finish threshing our granary. And disappointed she was not. Uncle commanded his eldest son, "Prepare yourself tomorrow to go and thresh the granary of your late uncle's children." Then as a gift to my little brother Hassoun, he sent with Imad one of the puppies spawned by their bitch Warda about two months ago. Uncle put an ornamented leather collar on the puppy's neck and gave it to Imad. Proud of the puppy, Imad returned and communicated the good news from uncle to mother. For the first time since father's death, we saw a tentative smile, albeit of gratitude, crossing her sorrowful, care-laden face. The puppy was chubby and had a beautiful white coat. Mother was happy with it, I think, even though she didn't show it. She simply told us to feed it well and to give it churned milk to drink, hoping that when he grows in strength and years he would protect our sheep from the wolves of the wilds.

From the trunk of our old clothes, we fished out a child's military uniform, with three stars on each epaulet, our father had bought for Hassoun the year before. Dressing the puppy in this uniform, Imad, Hassoun, and I took him

112

to show him off to the neighbors' puppy-less children. I think mother was not pleased with this deed, but she did not wish to deny her children a joy they badly missed since the passing away of their father, their breadwinner, their shepherd. One week later, our cousin brought the wheat bushels, and we had a good yield. We put our arms around mother, showered her with kisses, and begged her to grant us one wish. She asked us about it, but we made her promise to grant it first, and she did. Imad told her, "Do you remember how you used to boil wheat grains, gather the neighbors' children, and sprinkle the boiled grains on the head of the youngest among us to speed up his teething, while the other children pick up the falling grains and eat them after you sprinkle them with a pinch of salt?" She said, "Yes, I do. But I don't understand what you are driving at." Imad explained to her that we wanted her to boil a small pot of wheat grains, so that we could invite the neighbors' children, and throw the boiled grains on the head of our puppy Nammour. "God's will be done, brothers of Nammour!"

Mother's joke turned out to be like a prophecy. As soon as the neighbors heard about the boiled wheat party we threw in honor of Nammour, we were collectively called "The Brothers of Nammour" instead of "The Children of the Deceased." Later on, we heard that our mother was secretly nicknamed "The Mother of Nammour" by both my maternal uncle Khaddour, whom she had chased with a stick, and paternal uncle Sammour, who suddenly stood on his dignity and refused to finish threshing our granary.

In early autumn, temperatures began to drop at night. Coming back from school one Thursday afternoon, Imad and I decided to surprise our mother with something that would fill her empty heart with joy, or so we thought. The next morning, she went cotton-picking in the fields of uncle Haleem, and she left little Hassoun to play and have fun with us. Imad sent me to the neighbors to borrow a trowel and a wooden mortar for casting mudbricks, while he brought out a big sack of straw from the storehouse. We dug a pit in the middle of the compound near the summer sheep pen, piled the earth we dug out, spread the straw over it, and splashed it with about four buckets of water, which our mother used to carry from the river on the back of our she-donkey Dalla. We began to tread the pile with our bare little feet, as we have seen grownups do, and straw blades cut their tender bottom, especially when we stepped on a place hardly touched by water.

A strange wayfarer, heading west, was passing in front of our compound. He looked over the low wall, saw what we were doing, and asked us, "You're the brothers of Nammour?" We said we were and explained that we wanted to build him a hut to protect him from the cold of winter. The stranger said, "Well done and said." He offered to help us, so we welcomed and invited him. He didn't enter through the gate, but from a gap in the wall we and our neighbors use as a shortcut to each other's compound. He took off his jacket and socks, hung them on a nearby tree, tied his headdress round his neck, put on his plastic shoes, hiked his *thobe* and tied it round his waist, showing the posterior of his thighs from the depression of his knee joints to the lower creases of his buttocks.

He took the shovel from my brother's hand, shaped the pile of earth-and-straw mix like a basin, then poured into it two more buckets of water. Shoveling the semidry raised edge of the mix onto the water, he hobbled on around the basin, while the two masses of his buttocks were squirming rhythmically with his left foot on which he was pivoting. Stunned by this amazing dynamic symphony, we woke up only when suddenly we found ourselves face to face with the man's dark face instead of his white buttocks. He straightened his back, beaming with accomplishment, to adore his perfectly mixed pile of clay. He took a stick and drew a square on the level ground next to the little clay hill, then ordered me to sweep the loose earth and pebbles away. He picked up the wooden mortar, placed it in the extreme left corner of the square I have just swept, and shook it right and left to have a perfect fit between mortar and earth. Then he put in a bucket enough clay to make two bricks, poured it over the mortar, distributing it equally over the four corners, then pressed the poured clay with his ten fingers. Sprinkling a little water over the already moist clay, he picked up the trowel and quickly smoothed the surface of the mortar. Then he threw the extra clay back into the bucket. He waited about two minutes to allow the parched earth to suck a bit of the clay's moisture, and also in order for the bricks to have a harder consistency, as he explained to us. Then he gently loosened the mortar off the bricks and briskly jerked it clean. There stood before us two gorgeous bricks made of nothing but water, straw, and earth.

> Were the sun to humor us by sending her scorching rays during the day, and the skies by withholding their rains until the bricks are dried, we shall inaugurate our brother's residence next Friday. I can almost touch it with these hands of mine. Brother, it doesn't become Nammour to have no other bed but the earth and no other cover but the skies. What would uncle Haleem say were he to know that one of Warda's brood is mistreated at the hands of his late brother's own brood?

The stranger took the same stick, drew a crisscross of lines within the square I have swept, and showed my brother what to do with the rest of the clay. Taking a bucket of water, he began washing his hands, feet, and plastic shoes. In the meantime, Imad and I were busy making our next two bricks. We took no notice of the stranger's departure until Nammour bade him farewell—albeit with a shy, stifled woof—at the compound's western gate. My brother ran west, and I east, each jumping over the wall on his side, in a desperate attempt to redress our failure of duty. But the man slipped away like a genie into the bowels of the earth. Anyway, Nammour didn't lack manners or good breeding like us, for he thanked the stranger in his own way.

In vain we kept watching the horizon in search of the man. Suddenly we were gripped by a vague apprehension that didn't last long, for we heard Hassoun crying for help. We rushed back to him. He has slipped into the pit—his face, hair, and clothes all bespattered with mud. The poor kid was trying to remove the mud from his face and eyes but succeeded only in spreading it to other parts of his body. I picked up an empty bucket to bring water and wash Hassoun's face and hair, only to find that the stranger has used up our supply of water to the very last drop. We removed Hassoun's muddy clothes and tried in vain to wipe his face and hair with tattered rags, while he was crying his heart out.

At that very moment, there loomed the head of our she-donkey Dalla entering the compound, with mother riding her, both visibly exhausted. When mother saw Hassoun naked, in tears, and with a muddy face and hair, she beat her face and pulled her hair. She looked for water and found none. She saw the little pile of clay, the empty sack of straw, and figured our satanic plan. She leaped and threw both of us at the pile, pushing our faces deep into it, weeping and asking God in disbelief why she was repaid with brats like us. We wriggled out of her grip and ran, as if pulled by a mysterious power, towards the donkey's stall in the corner of the compound. When the donkey saw us running towards her and screaming, she was agitated and began kicking the air with her hind legs, and braying as if to warn our mother, "Beware of violating the sanctity of my dunghill or insulting anyone seeking asylum in it."

Much obliged, Mademoiselle Dalla!

In the end, mother had to calm down. Having made do with a simple spit on each one of us, she took Hassoun and stood him in front of the donkey who looked at him with pity. Leaving Hassoun in the care of the donkey, she went back to fetch the two big cylindrical barrels to bring us, before sunset, enough river water to tidy us up overnight. When my mother approached the donkey, she slung the two chained barrels over her back, which, in her fit of fury, she has forgotten to unsaddle. Neither the donkey protested, nor did mother care to justify this emergency mission to her companion in misery, as if each one of them has already forgotten her personal dispute with the other.

Mother returned from the river shortly before sunset. She lifted Hassoun off the back of the donkey, and he was quite clean in the face and hair. He was also decent not naked. She called Imad to come and help her carry the two barrels off the back of the donkey. Then she ordered that each one of us should take one bucket of cold water and bathe. All that evening, she remained silent. We expected her to explode any minute. That night we went to bed without supper. She neither offered any, nor did we dare to feel hungry. Before we went to bed, Imad whispered to me, "Do you know, Ghazi, that this evening we are poorer than we were this morning? We are short on one barrel of water, one sack of straw, one supper, and one mother's love. In our own front yard, we have dug a pit we know not which of us will fall into in the coming days." I didn't like his calculations.

Have a sack of straw, Imad!

Mother ordered us to leave the pile of clay, the pit, and the four bricks as they were. I think she wanted them to remain a nightmarishly concrete reminder of our own mismanagement. When I saw the shovel, perpendicularly stuck in the side of the clay pile, its handle raised in air, like an accusing forefinger, and pointing towards the gap from which the stranger had entered, I was certain of mother's intention. Two years passed and our dream of building a residence for Nammour remained unfulfilled. He lived just as other dogs in our village lived: on dry crumbs of bread and outdoors. He was no longer a cute puppy to fuss over. His coat of hair was yellowish and dirty. He was also afflicted with flies in summer and blood ticks in winter. He instinctively understood that this was his lot and he was contented.

Uncle Sammour failed so far to find a life-mate, and the repeated rejections ate his heart out. Neither the nubile maidens nor the unmarriageable spinsters accepted his proposals. He was rejected even by divorcees and widows. In fact if a suitor on his behalf came to any of them, she would viciously reply, "Oh, I'd rather hook up with a pair of shoes!" But he found a job as a municipal constable in Al-Adwaniyya, a village lying west of our own. The municipality had issued him a hunting rifle, a police uniform, and commissioned him to kill all dogs within the municipal borders, claiming they spread diseases and epidemics. Uncle Haleem shamed him for taking such a disgraceful job and advised him to quit. But how could he willingly surrender a convenient capacity that makes him fearsome, at least in the eyes of some villagers and their dogs? It occurred to him that charity begins at home, and so he wanted to start with Nammour. He hasn't set foot in our compound since he delivered his ominous ultimatum to our mother more than two and a half years ago.

He stormed the gate of our compound with an arrogant stride, his rifle slung over his shoulder, thinking himself le Général Gouraud when, from the outskirts of Damascus, he gave its inhabitants his famous ultimatum. He looked ludicrous in his police uniform. And to exercise the powers of his new job, he had to give up his *thobe, shimagh*, and *iqal*. Surprised by his visit, mother rushed to meet him. And like le Général Goybet, he addressed her, "Chère mère de Nammour, nous voilà de retour!" As soon as Nammour heard his name, he came barking. Sammour slung the rifle off his shoulder, broke it, pushed a cartridge in the chamber, and fired at Nammour but missed him. Nammour jumped over the wall and ran away, followed by Sammour. My mother rushed to the house, brought my late father's rifle, fitted a full magazine on it, and shouted at Sammour to stop chasing the dog, but he ignored her. Screaming Sammooooooour!, she fired one shot above his head. He tumbled like a beheaded chicken, his feet kicking the air, his rifle flung from his hand. Two wet spots began to form on the seat and crotch of his pants. Standing above him, mother spat on him and said, "I won't waste another shot on a varlet like you. Now get lost!" Actually, this last piece of advice was superfluous, for he got up, hung his head, and slunk away. He didn't even dare to ask mother to give him back his rifle.

In the afternoon, the mayor, accompanied by uncle Haleem, the village chief, and other notables, came to our house. Mother offered them tea, but they refused to drink it. Uncle Haleem addressed my mother, "Give us the spoils of war, noble sister of men!" To which she replied, "It is yours, on one condition!" He consulted with the mayor, the village chief, and the notables and asked her, "What's your condition, Om Imad?" She said, "Neither this nor any other rifle should be used to kill our dogs on the pretext of wanting to put an end to epidemics. We have lived with these dogs all our life, they watch over our homes and livestock, and they keep us company." The village chief scratched his little paunch, stuffed with churned milk and green onions, and mumbled, "Can't you find a better companion than dogs, Om Imad? Is there no one among us who is good for you?" She ignored him and asked the mayor, "What do you have to say about my condition?" For a few minutes, heads formed a new circle of consultations. Whispers and counter whispers were finally concluded by the mayor who announced, "In a desire to preserve civil peace in Al-Adwaniyya Municipality and the surrounding territories, it is thenceforward forbidden to use hunting rifles to kill dogs without the express approval of their owners, and that said dogs should be allowed to enjoy normal rights as before, including—nay, most supremely—the right to life." When the delegation of dignitaries left with the spoils of war, uncle Haleem spoke to my mother and commended her deed, saying, "Had you compromised your right to hold onto the rifle of your late husband, you wouldn't have achieved these gains for your fellow villagers." From then on, my mother was no longer nicknamed Om Nammour.

We looked for Nammour that evening and found him sulking among barren crags on the southern edge of the village. It was no easy matter persuading him to return to his home and family. When we came to the compound, mother offered him a dish of yoghurt and two hot loaves of bread. To entertain and comfort him, we staged a skit, roughly based on the day's events. Hassoun played Nammour, I played Sammour, the municipal constable, and Imad played mother. Imad and I carried two dry twigs and used them in place of rifles. I aimed my twig at Hassoun, who started running and woofing like a puppy, and I fired a "shot" at him. Frightened Hassoun so genuinely howled that he broke my heart; Imad, who was now my mother, screamed at me, "Sammoooooour!" Then I heard a "shot" pealing over my head. I fell on my back, kicking the air with my feet. Imad caught up with me, spat on me, and dragged me from my ear to where Hassoun was hugging Nammour. In the dimming light, it was hard to tell them apart from a distance. Imad made me kneel on all fours, offer my apologies, and vow repentance before Hassoun/ Nammour.

Figuring that we went beyond the call of duty in comforting any other dog within the municipal parameters of Al-Adwaniyya, we, now sleepy and exhausted, bade Nammour good night. The next morning, we were awakened by a strange barking within our compound. We called our mother, and when she didn't answer, we knew that she has gone to work in the fields. We were thus forced to get out of our beds to find out, and who do we see but the strange wayfarer holding a bitch the like of her has never been seen in our parts. We also noticed that he was not wearing the same type of clothes we saw him wearing the first time. He was now wearing a pair of pants, a shirt, and a hat. Not waiting for us to ask him what business brought him back to us after an absence of more than two years, he hastened to say, "Sorry to hear about what happened to Nammour." We thanked him, but perplexed questions kept whizzing in our heads. He read our minds and said, "I heard about the treacherous attempt at the life of your brother Nammour. Thanks to my knowledge of animal psychology, which I acquired during my travels in Western countries over the past two years, I can appreciate the impact of the emotional trauma such an assault has on the psychology of Nammour. In my last trip to Berlin, I bought this beautiful creature, named Amanda, who belongs to the noble pedigree of German shepherds. And here I come to place her at the disposal of Nammour. I think a few weeks with her are enough to make him forget the terrorism of kith and kin."

In addition to rolls of salivating bread, our friend produced rolls of dried meat and many other cans we have never seen before. From another bag, he took out a wide, clean plate, opened several cans, and poured their contents in it. Then he called Nammour who has been until this point completely oblivious to the presence of our two guests. When he saw the glamourous Nordic belle, with her shapely figure, he barked like someone who has just realized how much he missed out in life.

> Damn my bad luck! Proud daughter of dogs, where have
> you been all this time? And how did I not know you before?

The benevolent wayfarer invited Nammour and his new girlfriend to breakfast, telling us, "Let them break bread together." I wonder if there is such an expression in the language of khawajas, or whether they value such bonds of companionship. Anyhow, Nammour and Amanda broke bread together, and, man, you should really see how daintily she nibbled her breakfast. She would pick the morsel with the tip of her tongue, without once drooling like our embarrassing local dogs. In fact, only dignity stopped us from sharing their dainty meal, especially since we had no breakfast yet. All day long, they kept sniffing each other, frolicking, and galloping. When night came, and it was time for bed, well, I can't say what went on there, because, quite frankly, what went on between them requires post-coital ablution, assuming that dogs care about such purification rites. From dusk to dawn, they had such a blissful night unknown to us, supposedly superior human mortals. Getting up on the right side of Nammour, Amanda paced the compound to and fro like a queen checking up on her subjects, her ruffled coat of hair still showing visible signs of the previous night's amorous escapades.

We told our mother nothing about our guest. So while she was saddling Dalla, she was surprised to see this intruder pacing the compound as if she were in her own front yard. Waving at her, she said shoo!, but Amanda didn't yet know our language, not to mention the fact that as a matter of principle she rejects all shooing and the annulment of others. There is no problem that cannot be solved through negotiations; plus, "There is a place for all at the rendezvous of victory," selon Monsignor Aimé Césaire, may his bones rest in one piece. We tried all means to drive away this intruder and failed. We tried with Nammour, but he was totally blasé. Not only that, he no longer responded when we called him Nammour. Apparently, the fellow no longer likes this hillbilly name. But what should we call him? Romeo, for instance? Good lord, we no longer understand dogs.

The stranger kept bringing Amanda and her Romeo delicious supplies for two months or more. We also noticed that during the last days, he brought them only mutton chops and the tail fat of sheep. Suddenly, the stranger disappeared and all supplies came to an end. We went back to feeding Romeo whatever dry bread we could find, hoping he would regain his health in due time, but his mistress shared the few miserable morsels we threw him; indeed, she gulped most of them, and he didn't mind that much. It seems that after having tasted the good life, thanks to Amanda and her owner, he found our way of life too unpalatable.

One moonlit spring night, we were awakened by the persistent barking of Nammour. Accompanied by Imad, my mother snatched father's rifle and went out into the compound. She scouted every bit of it and found nothing suspicious. She counted the sheep in their pen and none was missing. Mother came back to bed, and her brief excursion revived her hope that Romeo would soon be the good old Nammour again. Apparently, he had sniffed a wolf around the pen and he chased him away from the sheepfold.

Near the gate of the sheep pen, we built him a mud hut, put a thatch roof on it, and furnished its floor with straw. We fished out whatever old clothes we no longer needed and spread them over the straw, and made him and his mistress, both now terribly emaciated, a comfy bed. Almost one week later, at night, we heard Nammour give out an ordinary woof at first, then his barking was suddenly stifled. My mother and Imad rushed out of the house to find out, and it looked to them that Nammour and Amanda were only foreplaying. They found nothing suspicious, and again no sheep was missing. We thanked God and began regaining our trust in Nammour. We also got used to Amanda in the meantime. After all, Nammour is no longer a puppy and thus has the right to choose his own mate. And if this mate happens to be a foreigner, so what!

Two days later, mother woke up at dawn and went to check upon the sheep. The bellwether was missing. Shucks, we haven't heard a single woof all night long! Oh, the bellwether must be hiding somewhere, or perhaps he jumped into the neighbors' compound. She looked and looked but found him neither in our compound nor in that of our neighbors. Suddenly, Nammour and Amanda came swinging through the western gate of the compound, their muzzles stained with blood. My mother ran towards them, and when she approached, Nammour greeted her with a burp. She was certain then that Nammour had gorged himself on fat and meat. But neither individually nor collectively could Nammour and Amanda kill the bellwether. We wanted to kill Nammour and his mistress with the rifle of our late father, but our mother objected.

At night my mother and Imad kept vigil in a hut near the sheep pen, hoping to unravel Nammour's mystery. At about 4:00 am, she saw a wolf, silhouetted in the moonlight, enter the pen, grab a two-year old sheep, and hightail out of the compound. Nammour and Amanda did not turn a hair; instead they slipped out of their love nest and followed the wolf to beyond the railroad passing north of our village. Imad wanted to follow them, but mother whispered that he should wait. Almost an hour and a half later, Nammour and his mistress wobbled back, their muzzles again stained with fresh blood. Mother accosted him, "Well, hullo there!" He greeted her back with an insolent burp. Mother swung her rifle, fired one single shot, but missed him. He ran away, howling. As for Amanda, well, she too howled and howled, as if to condemn this unjustifiable terrorism. She kept up her dirge of protests at a tempo unknown in our local dogs. And this was the first time we had the honor of hearing the voice of Amanda, our own sister in law.

A Message from the Sponsors

I NVITED TO TAKE PART IN AN EVENING SYMPOSIUM on environmental protection, he started getting ready for this occasion about two hours before the event. This was during the last days of winter, which usually never bids us farewell except with a surge of bitter cold weather. But the farewell this year was the harshest ever, as if all the winds of the earth rose against us.

"Should I take a shower or not? I should! Since when do I dither about a trifle like this?"

He carried the small electric heater into the bathroom, placed it on the ledge of the tub, plugged it into the socket, and turned on the faucet to fill the oblong tub with hot water. He closed the door and came to the bathroom foyer to brush his teeth and shave, leaving the hot steam and heater to comfort the walls of the bathroom with their warmth and assure them that this frosty wave would last only a brief spell. The walls of the bathroom were covered with deluxe mosaic tiles forming a semi-natural panorama of trees, roses, a serenely flowing brook, and a corpuscular, bloodshot sun inching out of the southeastern corner of the bathroom right above the ledge of the tub.

In front of the mirror, he stood in a serene, self-satisfied mood, reviewing his prospective after-shower handsomeness and what he would say to his audience in about two hours from now, and how he would start his talk: Should he start with a light joke to make his audience eager to hear what he would say next? Should he deliver his speech standing or sitting? Should he walk among his audience to vaunt his head-turning height among les belles dames—he hoped his audience would include some beautiful ladies interested in environmental protection—or should he slump like an old sweater on his comfy chair? Ah, would the chair be comfy or just a sloppy mishmash of sticks hurriedly put together and so wickedly designed as not to tempt a sitting speaker to bore the hell out of his audience with a prosaic speech-a-thon.

These mental meanderings—and how he would face his audience—occupied him about five or six minutes, but he could lay none of them to rest. He was through with brushing his teeth and shaving, and had thus no more reason to postpone storming the bathroom which must be ready by now to welcome a fine orator like him in all his captivating nakedness. He smelled something resembling the aroma of roasted meat, and there also came to his ears a barely audible cracking, accompanied by a prolonged, muted groan. Storming the bathroom, his nose met a strange roasting smell. He was apparently absentminded when he had placed the heater on the ledge of the tub. By putting it too close to the just rising sun from the southeastern corner of the bathroom, a great number of the small mosaic pieces were burned, the intense heat cracking their glossy enamel and roasting the red dry clay underneath. The roasted, steam-saturated mosaics were now dripping bright red tears into the water. The heat had also singed the tree leaves and roses with its searing glow.

He hurriedly showered and got dressed. He received a text message from the sponsors of the symposium saying, "Dear Sir, due to the severe weather conditions, we have decided to cancel this evening's symposium. We thank you for your cooperation and understanding."

V
NOTES

Acknowledgments & More

Acknowledgments

A Sojourner Reporting from Amman was the first story I wrote in 2002, I think, while the last one, "In Memory of Yousef," was written in October 2018. The former was the result of frustration with state bureaucracy and nepotism in Syria, the latter the result of disillusionment with the so-called Syrian opposition. In a bizarre way, I must thank both the deputy minister who inspired me to write "Sojourner," and the hypocritical nephew of my friend Yousef who inspired me to write "Yousef." In between, many other equally vicious instigators served as my personal muses.

However, there are good friends who deserve my heartfelt gratitude for their encouragement and inspiration. My first thanks go to Musa Rahum Abbas, whose collection of stories White Carnations (Cune Press) I had the pleasure to translate from Arabic.

The painter and sculptor Hassan Hamam provided the sketches for this book. For our cover, he also allowed us to sample a powerful painting he created that shows men, women, and children leaving their ruined town with sacks on their backs . . . and walking into the desert. A graduate of the College of Fine Arts, Damascus University, Hassan has been living and working in Riyadh, Saudi Arabia since 2000.

Other writers from my native town of Raqqa encouraged and inspired me as well. Now they are scattered all over the world: Ayman Nasser (novelist, painter, and sculptor), Maabad Alhassoun (journalist, historian, and novelist), and Ahmad Khamis (novelist). There are many others, of course, who also use their pens to fight for the cause of their people.

In addition, my sincerest thanks go to Dr Marream Krollos for proofreading the typescript, to Dr Omar Imday for providing a preface to the collection. Scott C. Davis, my publisher, deserves my utmost gratitude for believing in my writing and for his constant support.

For more:
Hassan Hamam, illustrator:
(https://www.facebook.com/hassan.hamam.9)

Cune Press

CUNE PRESS WAS FOUNDED IN 1994 to publish thoughtful writing of public importance. Our name is derived from "cuneiform." (In Latin cuni means "wedge.")

In the ancient Near East the development of cuneiform script—simpler and more adaptable than hieroglyphics—enabled a large class of merchants and landowners to become literate. Clay tablets inscribed with wedge-shaped stylus marks made possible a broad inter-meshing of individual efforts in trade and commerce.

Cuneiform enabled scholarship to exist, art to flower, and created what historians define as the world's first civilization. When the Phoenicians developed their sound-based alphabet, they expressed it in cuneiform.

The idea of Cune Press is the democratization of learning, the faith that rarefied ideas—pulled from dusty pedestals and displayed in the streets—can transform the lives of ordinary people. And it is the conviction that ordinary people, trusted with the most precious gifts of civilization, will give our culture elasticity and depth—a necessity if we are to survive in a time of rapid change.

Aswat: Voices from a Small Planet (a series from Cune Press)

Looking Both Ways	Pauline Kaldas
Stage Warriors	Sarah Imes Borden
Stories My Father Told Me	Helen Zughraib

 Syria Crossroads (a series from Cune Press)

Leaving Syria	Bill Dienst & Madi Williamson
Visit the Old City of Aleppo	Khaldoun Fansa
The Dusk Visitor	Musa Al-Halool
Steel & Silk	Sami Moubayed
The Passionate Spies	John Harte
The Road from Damascus	Scott C. Davis
A Pen of Damascus Steel	Ali Ferzat
White Carnations	Musa Rahum Abbas
Stories My Father Told Me	Helen and Elia Zughaib

 Bridge Between the Cultures (a series from Cune Press)

Confessions of a Knight Errant	Gretchen McCullough
Afghanistan & Beyond	Linda Sartor
Apartheid is a Crime	Mats Svensson
Arab Boy Delivered	Paul Aziz Zarou
Congo Prophet	Frederic Hunter
Music Has No Boundaries	Rafique Gangat

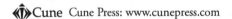

Cune Cune Press: www.cunepress.com

Born in the eastern countryside of the Syrian province of Raqqa, the erstwhile capital of ISIS, Musa Al-Halool has been a professor of English and Comparative Literature at Taif University, Saudi Arabia, since 2002. He is also a well known and prolific literary translator in the Arab world with nearly forty titles to his name. He traveled to the United States in 1989 on a Fulbright scholarship, where he obtained his MA and PhD in Comparative Literature from Penn State University in 1991 and 1995.

After returning to Syria, Musa Al-Halool taught at Tishreen University for four years before leaving for Jordan, where he taught for three years, and from there to Saudi Arabia. In 2016, ISIS declared him an "apostate" and requisitioned both his country house and in-town home in Raqqa.

It was in Jordan that Musa Al-Halool started writing short stories and poems in English. Afterward, he began writing in Arabic. He depicts ordinary folk with sympathy. His targets in government and the crony government economy, the corrupt, the arrogant, the mediocre, and the sycophantic—he skewers.

Musa Al-Halool's translations include *White Carnations* by the distinguished Syrian novelist and academic Musa Rahman Abbas (co-translated with Dr Sanna Dhahir), Cune Press 2021.

Select Books by Musa Al-Halool
Anguished Arabic (criticism in Arabic)
From the Herb of Burzoy to the Serpent of Gligamesh: Reflections on Literary Translation. (translation criticism in Arabic)
Exodus to Istanbul (travelogue in Arabic)
Literary Translation: Practical Applications in Translating Prose (a bilingual textbook)
A New Grammar for the New World Order (poems, short stories in English)
Bellweatheristan (a collection of short stories in Arabic)

CPSIA information can be obtained
at www.ICGtesting.com
Printed in the USA
JSHW050233040322
23348JS00001B/4